A New Beginning: Book Three

These Thousand Days

Other Books by Steven G. Hightower

A New Beginning: Book One
The Smoke of One Thousand Lodge Fires
An Amazon #1 Best Seller
https://www.amazon.com/dp/B08H9MXFGW/

A New Beginning: Book Two
The Cross of One Horse
An Amazon #1 Best Seller
https://www.amazon.com/dp/B09H4SF2Y1/

To: Buck
Thank you enjoy!

A New Beginning: Book Three

These Thousand Days

Steven G. Hightower

A NEW BEGINNING, BOOK 3
These Thousand Days
Copyright © 2022 Steven G. Hightower

ISBN: 978-1-7358416-5-6

All rights reserved. No part of this publication may be reproduced or transmitted in any form or by any means, electronic, mechanical, photocopying, recording, or otherwise, without written permission from the publisher. Published by Little Creek Publishing Co.™ Contact sales@littlecreekpublishingco.com.

This is a work of fiction. Any references to historical events, real people, or real places are used fictitiously. Other names, characters, places, and events are products of the author's imagination, and any resemblance to actual events, or places, or persons, living or dead, is entirely coincidental.

Library of Congress Control Number: TXu 2-308-223

For more information about Steven G. Hightower, visit
www.stevenghightower.com or Facebook.com/anewbeginning2020

Front cover image © Dreamstime 130871192 © Chris Hartman

*This book is dedicated to my children,
Jason and Jessica.
You have made our lives full and richly blessed.
Thank you.*

Chapter 1

Topusana
My Dreams
From the Year 1837

We were starving. I had experienced hunger many times in my life walk. I had intentionally fasted for days during my training under the guidance of Tosahwi. Today was different. The buffalo had simply disappeared into the vastness of the frozen prairie.

Our Band had departed the San Saba in beautiful warm autumn weather. This had been the rhythm and pattern of our life for centuries. We wintered in the southern plains, spent our summers in the north, then followed the buffalo herds farther north in the autumn, harvesting and preserving the meat for winter. It was a blessed way of life, The NuMuNuu (*The People*) living, existing with the provision of the Great Spirit and the bounty of Mother Earth. We lived in and upon a land of plenty, a land filled with game of all kinds. Deer, turkey, rabbit, quail, and grouse were in abundance. Fish filled the rivers and streams. Native pecan and walnut trees grew massive along the banks of the rivers within our homelands. We even grew crops—corn, beans, and squash—along the lowland river bottoms. Our primary food, however, was buffalo. The buffalo herds provided nutrition, tools, and even shelter. We used the hides of these incredible animals for our great tepee lodges.

With the invasion of the white man into our lands, much had changed. War had come. Survival was becoming difficult. But this was different. The buffalo were, unbelievably, becoming impossible to find. How could this be? How could millions of animals vanish?

Deep in my spirit I knew the answer to these questions. My mind was simply not ready to acknowledge what my spirit knew. The buffalo, like *The People,* were being eliminated.

As we moved along the frozen prairie, I had no way of knowing the disappearance of the buffalo herds was intentional. Part of a military plan was to remove our food source, thus removing all *The People*. We had been faithful stewards of the earth for centuries. What I did know this day was hunger. Each person, old, young, warrior, mother, and father alike suffered as one. My daughter, Prairie Song, and the other young ones suffered most. They could not understand. They felt the hunger pangs like all *The People.*

"Mommy, do you have just a bite of meat?"

I had answered and offered tiny pieces of meat to her daily. For weeks now, she seemed content with the small portion of dried buffalo, but today nothing was left. *"Perhaps, today Father will find the buffalo, Prairie Song. You must be strong. The Great Spirit will provide for us soon."* I saw the confusion in her eyes. I saw the weakness and suffering in her drawn, frail body. We would break camp tomorrow and move farther north. For now, the wind blew fierce against the lodge. The cold permeated everything. I reached for the water container only to find its contents a frozen block of ice even within the relative warmth of the teepee lodge.

These Thousand Days

"Come to me, Prairie Song." We snuggled together under the warmth of the huge buffalo hide. The thought occurred to me…this might be how we perish. I would make my only daughter as comfortable as possible if these were to be our last days. I drew my long knife and ran its sharpened edge along my inner thumb. I squeezed my hand repeatedly…finally the blood began to flow. I offered my thumb to my starving daughter. She began to suckle the small amount of blood. How could a mother prevent the starving of her child? I prayed again, the desperate prayers born only from the love within a mother's heart.

Prairie Song sighed—a tiny sound of comfort at the taste and nourishment from the blood that flowed from my body. Then she fell into a deep sleep.

The vision came to me suddenly. My heart and soul were relieved at what I saw. Just one more day, one more day of frozen water, frozen toes, and no food. Tomorrow the Great Spirit would answer our prayers. I drifted into a restless sleep filled with the smells of roasting buffalo. The tastes of the delicacies their bodies would provide floated within my dreams. The aroma of marrow stew seasoned with wild onion, tender cattail root, and watercress lingered in my mind. The vision of my daughter's belly swelling graced my dreams. I saw her face once again smiling. I awakened occasionally hoping, wishing, praying I had seen correctly.

Chapter 2

My Dreams

Tabbananica (Voice of the Sun), my husband, along with his friend Neeko (One who Finds) were considered saviors and rightly so. The two had succeeded in their hunt under the most difficult conditions imaginable.

We had camped along the frozen creek for one full moon cycle. The wind had been brutal for weeks. The small amount of ice and snow that had fallen, along with temperatures that must have been near zero for days, had frozen the prairie into an ice pack. Even venturing out of the lodges for a few small pieces of wood was life threatening. During the wind storms a person might become disoriented and easily lose sight of the camp. If that occurred, one simply would not survive. We needed food and wood fuel. If the Warriors failed, our entire Band would perish. This was known…but never spoken.

In these brutal conditions, the men had departed for the hunt each day. The footing was difficult for both the men and the ponies. They carried with them those stark facts of what was known. They carried upon their shoulders the lives of one hundred or more good and faithful souls.

As the sky lightened in the east to a dull low overcast with a constant biting wind and a driving frozen rain, Tabba, as I referred to my husband, dressed and prepared for the hunt.

"*You will find the buffalo today, husband,*" I said.

"*I will do my best, Sana.*"

"*Understand, husband. I have had a dream. I have seen clearly. The buffalo will be huddled on the earth. Drive the lance deep. We will feast tonight.*" His eyes brightened at my words. I peered into those eyes and saw a hope I had not seen in days. "*We will break camp today and move to a more protected location. I have seen this also. Maguara will give the order this day.*"

As he turned and opened the teepee flap, I saw a newfound resolve on his face. I offered all of who I was as his woman, all that a man might dream of and hope for.

"*You will be full and warm this night, Tabba. And you will also have me as your wife. Save a little bit of your strength this day. It will be needed for what I have planned for you under the buffalo robe.*"

I kissed him passionately. I had never been this forward with my man. His steps as he strode through the camp toward the war ponies revealed a purpose and driven intention. I prayed again I had seen correctly.

****

That night the fires burned brightly within the teepee lodges. The men had returned late in the day, their war ponies loaded with buffalo meat. My vision proved true and correct.

I was incredibly grateful. My gifting was becoming clearer. I knew and was beginning to see more of our future. Much of what I saw, however, I did not desire to see.

These Thousand Days

Prairie Song and I, along with *The People,* moved several miles that morning. We set up camp below a bluff along a frozen creek bottom. Enormous cottonwood trees lined the creek bank, their limbs stripped by the wind of even the old leaves that sometimes cling to their branches through the harsh winter. Much fuel wood had fallen from these life-giving trees. We easily gathered enough wood for days of lodge fires.

That night as *The People* feasted, the story of the hunt was told around each lodge fire. Laughter drifted within the camp, along with the intoxicating smell of meat roasting. As the darkness settled across the prairie, the families made their way into the safety and warmth of each tepee lodge. Prairie Song drifted off to sleep, her little belly swollen and filled with the nutritious marrow and pure meat.

Under the soft warm buffalo robe, I gave myself to my man completely. In ecstasy and gratefulness, I overflowed, in every sense I possessed, with pleasure and blessing. As I lay in the arms of Tabba, I wondered how the circumstance of life could change so quickly. Just a few hours ago, we were not certain we would survive. Now we were filled with the blessings of life, love, hope, and food provided by Mother Earth.

Hours later I lay awake, caught up in thought and prayer. I breathed a deep sigh of relief. My movement and sound awakened Tabba. He reached for me yet again…warm and strong.

Chapter 3

My Dreams

That season we took only five buffalo during the fall hunt. It would not be enough. We processed every usable part of the glorious animals. We feasted daily, gaining much needed strength. Two weeks passed before the sun finally showed itself. The frozen prairie welcomed the soft warmth that grew each day, as did *The People*. However, even with the warming of the prairie, a cloud of worry and doubt hung over our days.

Our Warriors and hunters never imagined not finding the massive herds of buffalo that roamed the plains each fall. This was a disturbing sign to all. I realized for the first time during that fall hunt that we as a people would never survive the invasion of our homeland. Our way of life, our culture, our families, like the buffalo, were in danger of extinction.

The council met the night prior to our departure south. I was included in these talks. Our Chief, Maguara, understood what many in the past had not—the voice of wisdom spoke often through the women of our Band. Maguara was a wise leader. The plan would be the same as it had been for centuries. We would once again move south for the winter months. This would be the first time we had done so as a people with no winter food supply gained from our movement north.

The fire burned brightly within the sacred circle. The conversations were not hurried or rushed. Each person took time with their words. Thinking before speaking in our culture was prized and showed wisdom on the part of the speaker. I sat in silence, listening. I understood the need to move on. This would solve several problems. But I knew we faced a greater problem than a food shortage. The smoke from the sacred pipe rose and mingled with the wood smoke. I stood to speak.

"*The plans of Maguara are good. Our men will continue to harvest the deer as we travel. The women will be successful in gathering the grouse, rabbit, and quail. The Comanche must adapt to survive, and we will.*" I paused but remained standing.

"*Topusana has seen other things?*" Maguara questioned.

"*Yes.*" A new quiet fell within the sacred circle. The fire crackled, breaking the silence. A wolf began to call from far across the prairie. Somewhere within the dark night came the reply of his mate. Breathing deeply, I gazed at Tabba. I wanted to remember this moment and these many days in which I had been so blessed to live out and walk. I cherished these thousand days I had lived that resembled the scene before me now, for I knew these days were coming to an end. The lodge fires would eventually fade. The buffalo would disappear from the prairie. Many tribes would perish and vanish from the earth just as the buffalo would.

"*We must escape. The scarcity of the buffalo is a sign for all. They will soon disappear from the prairie. This is but the beginning…of our ending. The Comanche are in grave danger, and we must escape.*" My words were met with a chorus of gasps and muffled disbelief.

Tosahwi rose and stood beside me. "*The words of Topusana are true and correct, my brothers.*" Again, a crescendo of grumbles and gasps drifted faintly into the smoke from the lodge fire.

The words I had spoken also rose into the heavens as they mingled within the cloud of smoke, rising both as a plea and a prayer to our Creator.

I stood in silence before the leaders of our people. "*Where might* The People *possibly escape this army of whites that kill the buffalo and invade even the Llano?*" Maguara asked, a look of doubt showing on his face.

"*We have no place to escape on this earth. Anywhere we may go the whites will pursue us.*" I paused. "*Our only hope of survival as a people is to escape into the* Dream Time."

My suggestion was met with a loud and raucous flurry of comments. Some wanted to stay and fight to the last man, woman, and child. Others felt we should not change one thing about our daily lives, that to do so would be seen as cowardly. Still others simply denied the possibility of millions of animals dying or being killed. But I knew what I had seen, however unlikely or impossible it may have seemed to my friends and family gathered around this sacred fire…I knew what I had seen was true.

Tosahwi, standing beside me, spoke words of wisdom that penetrated the hearts of even those most opposed to my suggestion. "*Listen well, my brothers and sisters, the* Dream Time *may spare even a remnant of our people if what Topusana has seen comes to pass. We must consider but one question… Shall we all perish?*"

His question ended any further discussion. "*Tomorrow as we break camp and travel across what has been ours since the beginning of time, let my question burn in your hearts and minds. Shall we all perish?*"

Chapter 4

My Dreams

After we had traveled seven days toward the south, the prairie eventually became free of ice and snow. This seemed to lift the spirit of *The People*. We had endured the cold and near starvation in our quest to find the buffalo. The warming weather and our bodies being nourished by the pure buffalo meat revived us in countless ways. As we traveled, the walking became much easier. I traveled near the rear of our procession along with the other mothers who carried their infants. Children old enough to walk did so, the *Old Ones* also traveled with us near the rear of our Band.

The movement under these conditions was a wonderful bonding time for all. Relationships were nurtured; conversations were unhurried and intimate. The *Old Ones* shared songs as they walked along. Some days the songs rose in unison as the tune was taken up by the entire Band. For days and many seasons, we sang our way across the prairie as we moved upon Mother Earth.

At nightfall around our evening fires, the *Old Ones* told their tales of past victories. Young maidens whispered to one another concerning their admiration and attraction to the young Warriors. The young men likewise sat at a distance, ribbing one another at the occasional glance of a maiden in their direction. It was a blessed time.

The Warriors scouted one or two days ahead of our Band. This served several purposes, the most significant being it provided a level of security. The Comanche had enemies, although several other tribes who opposed us in the past had in recent times become our allies. The white man was now the primary threat to every Native American tribe.

This day as we traveled along, Chief Maguara drifted toward the rear of the Band. He walked beside me in silence. I knew he wanted to talk. The young mothers, in respect, distanced themselves from us. The older ones stayed near. They would remain silent but listen intently.

"*Sana, do you believe the white man can be negotiated with?*" he asked. I did not respond immediately. Thinking of the past and the numerous failed negotiations, I answered with a question.

"*The men who now hold what they refer to as the Republic of Texas desire a treaty?*" I asked. He gazed into my eyes with a knowing look and nodded.

"*Sam Houston is an honest and true man. I discerned it in his eyes,*" he replied.

"*I am certain your observation is correct, my chief. However, you must consider the fact that most whites oppose him.*"

He lowered his gaze toward our feet then stared ahead. I knew he desired a diplomatic resolution to the invasion of our lands. Maguara still held out hope. Hope that a treaty might be agreed to and honored. In my heart I hated to dampen the hope he held. Maguara was a mighty, brave, and honest man. He led our people from the perspective of a servant. I loved and admired him in many ways. I spoke quietly to him.

"Perhaps Buffalo Hump can also offer advice concerning possible negotiations." My grandfather Buffalo Hump was the leader of the entire Penateka Band of Comanche, and I knew he had determined to never negotiate with the white man again. Maguara also knew this.

Chief Maguara peered intently into my eyes. He had received his answer. It was then I saw. A vision flashed across my mind in an instant. His hope would cost many lives.

"Thank you, Sana," he said. He strode forward with a wave directed at the mothers and children. I could see the weight he carried along and across the prairie. He was responsible for the lives that walked along beside us. We began to sing the song of our Creator, the song imparting knowledge and wisdom on those who seek Him.

****

The following day Tabba and the other Warriors rode into our group at breakneck speed. We all knew this could mean only one thing: danger lay ahead. It would take only minutes for the news to travel through the entire Band.

The mothers gathered their children as did I. Prairie Song clung to my skins at the news. White men lay in our path. I kept my hand on her shoulder, comforting her. But I felt the trembling of her little body at the news. As a mother, I hated that my child felt this level of fear at the mention of the white man. I hated seeing that same fear in the faces of the young mothers that surrounded me.

The council met immediately. *"These whites are trespassing on our sacred ground; they must pay with their lives,"* spoke my husband. Tabba was a fierce man and protector of our people. Positive grunts and replies emanated from others. The scouts reported the invaders numbered about twenty men.

Chief Maguara cleared his throat, then paused before responding. *"We could easily attack and kill most of these men. This will only bring more white men. The People are beginning to recover from our ordeal on the frozen plain. Perhaps in this instance we should evade these men. We are not well supplied; a pursuit would be difficult."* Several within the circle nodded in agreement. I prayed his wisdom might prevail. A quiet fell within the lodge while the men and Warriors passed the sacred pipe.

"The words of the great Chief are good words filled with wisdom. Let us move into the canyon to the north. By nightfall, the Comanche will surely disappear like the mist of late morning," Tabba said. I breathed a deep sigh of relief and nodded my approval in his direction. My man was fierce, and he was learning.

We did evaporate into the canyon land. We left no trace of our movement. The white men never even scouted in the direction of our movement.

My resolve was steeled again in the days that followed. We needed to escape…and we needed to prepare and plan our escape carefully, precisely, and intentionally. The *Dream Time* was powerful medicine, and it could transport us…hopefully into a time of peace.

Chapter 5

My Dreams

The winter of 1838 we set our camp in the center of the Llano, within the endless sea of grass. Here we would be safe. Most whites never attempted to enter or cross this massive expanse of land. We, as a people, knew what the whites did not know: within the Llano was life. Hidden springs flowed freely; little imperceptible valleys contained abundant wildlife. Deer, elk, even the occasional buffalo would feed our Band. It was a blessed winter, despite the unsuccessful buffalo hunt.

My daughter, Prairie Song, turned seven that year. What I remember more than anything about that season was she was happy. We all were happy. The threat to our way of life faded into the vastness of the blue sky and shining sun that graced this land. Our land.

But at night, the visions continued. The whites were coming. Like a wave of wind rolling across the prairie grass, I saw the waves of humanity rolling into our lands. I saw that we were an obstacle. We *The NuMuNuu* (The People) were in their way.

The following spring the runners arrived with news from the stronghold in the Llano. Buffalo Hump would attack. I could see fierceness and resolve in the eyes of our Warriors and in my own husband's eyes. The Texans would pay…and pay dearly.

One year later I held the hand of my daughter, Prairie Song, as we waved goodbye to our Warriors. They were proud and fierce and filled with resolve. The raiding party would travel south and east toward the great water where it was reported Texans were arriving daily. It was agreed the woman and children of our Band would stay behind. We had a safe, secure place to await their return…the cavern.

****

Just above the river San Saba was a small canyon. The slope was gradual and an easy climb from the river bottom. The entrance to the hidden cavern was a small opening in the ground. To those who did not know otherwise the entrance resembled an animal den, perhaps a wolf den or even a rabbit hole. We intentionally never enlarged the size of the entrance. To enter the cavern, it was necessary to crawl on hands and knees. Once inside a few feet, a sharp vertical drop required a climb down a steep slope.

At the bottom of that descent was bedrock. From there it was impossible to stand as the distance from the bedrock floor to the ceiling was less than three feet. We crawled along the cavern floor the morning the war party departed. The travel was difficult, possibly half a mile before the massive rooms opened before us. Live streams of fresh water flowed throughout the spacious cavern rooms. Enormous stalactites hung from the cavern ceiling. Boulders that had evidently fallen from above over the centuries littered the cavern floor. We worked our way, finally walking upright, along the little trail that led to the edge of a small lake. The torches we made from the tar pits above ground illuminated our way. From here we could make out the wall etchings. As the light from our torches danced upon the cave wall, the ancient etchings of our ancestors came alive.

Our people had left these stories upon the cavern walls centuries ago. This brought a level of safety and security to my mind. Knowing others had taken shelter and refuge here in this place…for eons…was comforting. Making our way into the elevated area where little side rooms had formed into the sandstone along the edges of the large cavern, we settled in.

About twenty of us stayed behind. Young maidens, a remnant of mothers with small children. Both boys and girls were intentionally chosen to accompany me. I unloaded my new supplies into the extensive cache with which we had previously supplied the cavern. I lit a fire, and its warmth brought our new home alive with light and comfort. The smoke hole, some seventy feet above us, gently drew the smoke upward into the Texas sky. I placed the medicine bag and scroll Tosahwi had created upon the rock shelf in my sleeping room. I prayed its contents would not be needed.

We would wait here within the cavern for no more than one moon cycle, thirty days. We had bead work and skins for making clothing. Our days would be good days. The time would be filled with conversation, prayer, lessons teaching the young ones from the scroll, and work for our hands to keep us occupied. We knew the mission of our Warriors was dangerous. I had seen nothing of the outcome. Our prayers would be numerous and sincere. If our men did not return within the allotted time frame, the outcome of their raid would be obvious. We would hold the sacred ceremony.

If the war party did not return within one moon cycle, this little remnant of survivors would enter the *Dream Time*. We would travel across the unknown into a time and place where we might attempt a new beginning.

Chapter 6

Topusana
Present Day
The Year 2070

I awakened from the same detailed dream that occasionally came to me. My past, the story of my life played out within another place in my mind where emotions were re-lived, a time where memories became real, where even senses blossomed to life…the touch of my man, the taste of roasted buffalo, the smell of the lodge fires. I breathed deeply, realizing it was just my dreams…again.

I turned on the light and stared at the painting as I lingered on the edge of my fading emotion. My heartbeat returned to normal. I closed my eyes, remembering. The recurring dream was not a nightmare. It was more like a friend that dropped by for an unexpected visit, detailing an intimate conversation with my past.

As I lay gazing at the painting in the early morning light, I realized again it must have been that day on the frozen prairie that the men had observed our movement. Karl Bodmer and his guide had watched us. They had seen the embrace as I held my daughter, comforting her in the best way I could.

Something about this troubled me. It was as if someone had invaded what was meant to be only ours. This precious time was not one that was to be shared with others, yet the existence of the painting Karl Bodmer created had played a key role in the future of my people.

The masterpiece, *Mother and Daughter,* now hung in the elegant room at the top of the stairway within the massive ranch house the Rosses had built. I peered again at the painting, my emotions and memories now fading within my heart and soul. I closed my eyes, not wanting those feelings to leave me so soon.

I loved to remember.

I was old now, nearing eighty I suppose. In the way most cultures or people count years I should have been frail and elderly. However, the *Dream Time* had an amazing mysterious physical benefit to those who traveled along its path. I am certain I still appeared as a woman in her late thirties or possibly forty. For lack of a better description, I felt extremely healthy and exceptionally fit.

I could still hunt, shoot the bow, take small game animals with a sling and stone. I could run for miles. My physical strength had never wavered in my eighty years on Earth. My mind and giftings had also sharpened and developed. I understood much. I could see and sense the motivations and intentions of men and women in positions of power within moments of speaking with them. The gift of discernment was invaluable, and I, Sana Nica, *Akima* (Leader) of our people, possessed this ability on a level never before known.

I was also quite skilled at concealing this gift. The gift of concealment remained a tool just as valuable to our people as discernment itself. Perhaps the two are separate giftings that work hand in hand. We had come to this time almost fifty years ago. I would like to say we lived in peace during those years. In truth, we had not.

The survivors, our little Band of Comanche had indeed escaped from the year 1844 into a new time, into a place on Earth where our new beginning would benefit us most. Our former Homeland along the quiet San Saba River was now again our home. Yes, it was a new beginning. However, the struggle to survive had continued. The same enemies rose against us. Their tactics in this new time were different, their ultimate goal the same. Those in positions of power still wanted, desired, even lusted after the land and its resources we had been given.

The second pandemic had been much more severe. The cities had literally emptied as the mass of humanity attempted to escape the condition that spread the virus most, that was simply living in close proximity to others. Living in a city became a death sentence for millions.

And so, they came. At first just the few who had gained minimal survival skills made their way into the remote wilds of the western United States. They traveled in pickup trucks and large SUVs, at least until their gasoline was gone. Eventually they traveled on foot. Most perished…unable to feed themselves or locate water or care for their sick. Most never made it beyond a remote highway or dirt road. The rare ones who did live found themselves pitted against one another. Those who survived these conditions and ensuing civil warfare eventually made their way to the boundaries of our Homelands. None would enter. Our Warriors made certain of this. Our land remained free from the virus…and those who attempted to carry it to us.

The settlement program I had initiated almost fifty years ago had been an overwhelming success. We had been granted the area formerly known as Big Bend National Park as our

Homeland. This land was rugged, remote, and empty. A grant bequeathed to us by the hand of the president of the United States, with congressional approval, added 800,000 acres to the more than 250,000-acre tract gifted to our tribe by my adoptive father David Ross. His friend and attorney William Travis continued throughout his lifetime to add to our land holdings. Over the years, William Travis had become my closest friend and ally. I missed him terribly. His was a good death.

Together we had drafted and implemented the settlement program. Our Homelands were now populated with thousands of true, pure Native American Comanche and Apache families. Fierce, independent, self-sustaining, we lived free upon Mother Earth.

The buffalo herd had grown into the hundreds of thousands. They were no longer in danger of extinction, as they had been in my former life—the life and time we had escaped.

The painting of me with Prairie Song had exquisitely captured our intimate loving embrace. The masterpiece kept our former life in perfect focus. I would never forget what men were capable of…nor what they were attempting yet again.

Chapter 7

The Year 2070
San Saba Reservation

Our Homeland was governed as an independent nation. We had been granted federal trust protection and sovereign nation status, due to the actions of our friends working at the Bureau of Indian Affairs in Washington DC. We were not subject to the laws of the United States. At the angst of many, we developed the resources of Mother Earth. In my role as Akima, the US government opposed every decision I made.

The United States sued us, attempted to tax us, and over the decades sent innumerable violent protesters to our gates. The media giants followed the marching orders of those in power and dutifully ran their biased news reports daily. Those in power were determined to destroy our nation while attempting to retake what was rightfully ours. This government action against *The People* was nothing new. We had faced this enemy in the past. We, as a people, if forced, would fight in a new way. I would never waver in my defense of our Homeland and our precious people. And due to the recommendations, advice, and wisdom of my friend and tribal attorney William Travis and Tosahwi, our Shaman, we were prepared, more prepared than any adversary the United States government might ever face.

I had over the last nine days just completed a long overdue tour of our Homeland. We had traveled as we would have in the past, by horseback. It was the most advantageous way to view and observe both the progress, the condition of the land, and to meet and speak with our people.

My husband, Tabba, led the way, my sons William and David following near him. Little Abigail and I always close behind. Tosahwi and Tenahpu brought up the rear of our procession on their beautiful mares. Our mounts were bred from the descendants of the stallion Shadow. The bloodline was pure, strong, and unmatched in confirmation, ability, and the raw speed and agility of a true war pony. The animals were born on this prairie and as at home upon this land as we were. The time we spent on this outing was indeed a treasure.

We had invested wisely. The monies from oil production and a previous enormous lump settlement of $200,000,000 from the State of Texas had been used to build our independence, energy independence primarily. We reached the refinery on the evening of our first day of travel. It appeared from miles away. The emission stacks reaching into the evening sky. There were no plumes of foul air emitted from the plant. We used the latest technology developed by our own Native engineers. The process was clean and efficient. We stopped upon a small rise, observing; the refinery was surrounded by hundreds of thousands of trees. The simple logic employed was remarkable, those trees soaked in atmospheric carbon dioxide, and in turn those trees produced pure clean oxygen. This process left the heavens of Mother Earth surrounding the refinery, pure and clean.

"The output is up to eighty thousand gallons per day now, Mother," David said. The small refinery we built churned out the fuel daily, gasoline, diesel, even jet fuel. The EPA had been successful in shutting down every refinery in the United States. They had attempted the same actions against our refinery…unsuccessfully. We were, in spite of the desires of the governmental agents, not subject to the rulings of the EPA.

Due to our expert legal defense team that my son David now led, we had never lost a case concerning our status as a Sovereign Independent Nation.

"And the price today?" I questioned.

"Just over five hundred dollars per gallon," David replied.

Prices for our products had soared over the last four decades. The dependance on foreign energy had bankrupted the United States, while we grew energy sales into the trillions. It was not difficult to reach that level of sales at the current market price.

We camped that night within the tree covered forest land surrounding our refinery. I was amazed at the efficiency of the noise suppressors. I listened to the faint call of the night birds surrounding our camp. Mother Earth seemed happy. She knew her children were using her resources responsibly, just as our people had for thousands of years.

I awakened the following morning in the pre-dawn starlight. A light wind whispered in the tops of the pecan orchards. I wandered several hundred yards from our little camp and settled near a wide free-flowing stream. Water flowed within our homelands everywhere now. I entered my time of quiet, reflecting on the unbelievable discovery. In our exploration for oil, we had stumbled upon a hidden resource I knew in my heart would become more valuable than even the oil and natural gas reserves we developed. We had discovered an ocean of fresh clean water.

I felt his presence in the dim light of the breaking dawn. He held his hand high, his palm open to me. I returned the gesture. Tabba moved toward me silently and seated himself near me. We listened as the gift of a new day dawned before us.

The deer began to move toward the water; a rabbit stirred in the grass; the fish began to make little swirls in the waters of the stream. The birds began to sing.

"I am proud of you, Sana; do you hear what I hear?" he questioned. *"What The People have built under your leadership…is causing Mother Earth to sing."* We joined her in the morning songs of life. Water had brought life to much of what was formerly desolate.

****

In a remote area of the Big Bend, test oil wells had been drilled. There was not a significant amount oil, but our Native geologist began to put together a pattern of what seemed was a field of water. In the first few years, it did not seem that unusual to hit water in the test holes. But the deeper we drilled the cleaner and more pristine the water samples became. It took several years to define the ocean of fresh water that lay deep within Mother Earth, but it was there. Below the surface of the dry desert landscape of the Big Bend we discovered a literal sea of fresh clean water.

We strode hand in hand back to our little camp, our hearts full from our time of quiet among the trees. William served us a delicious breakfast of fire grilled trout and poached quail eggs. "We should make the power station by noon, Mother," he said. I nodded.

We mounted our ponies and set out to cover the twenty plus miles. Our mounts took to the task with enthusiasm. This exploration seemed to awaken all our spirits, both human and animal.

With the profits from the refinery revenue, we built our own power grid. At the heart of the system was an underground natural gas-fired electrical generating station. We reached the site of the generating station that afternoon. From above ground, there was no indication the underground plant even existed. The earth provided the clean energy needed to power the massive turbines. It took years to complete the transmission lines, which were also constructed underground. Even the most remote areas of our Homeland were supplied with clean efficient electricity.

We sat our mounts directly above the massive underground plant. The sky overhead was a clear pearl blue. I heard the call of a red hawk soaring high in the afternoon sky. It was simply amazing that under our ponies' hooves millions of kilowatts of electricity were being generated. The team had seen our arrival. Tosahwi led the way down a small arroyo. We dismounted as a ten-foot section of the cliff face before us opened wide. We were greeted by Shaa' (Sun), the remarkably gifted leader of our engineering team.

"*Welcome, Topusana*," Shaa' greeted our delegation in her native Apache language. The natural beauty of the woman radiated from her countenance. We spent the remainder of our day exploring the massive project. Her amazing intellect paired with her ability to explain the system in simple terms was fascinating.

That night as I lay in the underground sleeping rooms, my mind wandered again into our past. Our abilities as a people to live in another time without the modern world technologies of electricity, fuels, and agriculture was an indication of our strong will to adapt and survive.

This is what we were witnessing as we toured our Homeland. The will of *The People* to adapt and not just survive…but to adapt and thrive…just as we had in our past.

The following morning, we mounted our ponies. It would take three days of travel to reach our next destination, the center of our agricultural development in the wide-open spaces of the Big Bend. Those three days of travel, however, transported us into a different time.

Around noon that day, we spotted them roaming wild and free. Within another hour we rode within an unbelievable wave of life. The buffalo. Tens of thousands of the magnificent animals grazed in the deep lush grass of the prairie. They waded belly deep into the lakes and ponds that dotted the surface of our land. We set camp amidst the throng of life that had sustained us for centuries.

The herd did not seem to notice the young bull my father, Tenahpu, took silently with his ancient bow. Each in our party took part in the processing of the beautiful animal.

We gathered around the sacred fire that evening, partaking of the most prized and delectable cuts from the animal. Roasted buffalo tongue and buffalo hump. The meal satisfied our natural cravings for the food of our ancestors. I felt as if we had been transported into our past. It was as Tosahwi stated, *"A good day."*

I agreed, although blessed day may have been a better description.

The remainder of our journey to the south and west proved to be just as exhilarating and wonder-filled as the beginning of our travel.

Late into the third day of travel from the power plant, we could make out the most impressive development our people had undertaken, our agricultural development. The farmland rolled ahead of us for dozens of miles.

Many of our young people were incredibly bright and creative. They were schooled in engineering, design, arts, and industry. Tribal members attended the finest agricultural colleges and engineering schools. The results of their training and dedication, along with unlimited resources, produced the agricultural envy of the world. In the fertile desert valleys of the Big Bend, we grew the finest crops in the United States, including wheat, corn, soybeans, berries, melons, and more. The earth blossomed year-round with orchards bursting with citrus, avocado, pecan, almond—an immeasurable bounty. We harvested millions of tons of food annually. The land, it seemed, had waited for centuries to produce its incredible harvest. The desert floor, rich in minerals, once irrigated with the sweet water hidden deep underground, produced what were the finest crops ever grown.

We entered the fields of wheat that rolled along beyond our vision.

"The crop is pre-sold again this season?" my son William asked.

"Yes, brother," my son David replied to our entire group. *"The provinces of Russia are once again desperate to feed their people. The contract I drafted myself will feed them for years, but more importantly retain them as an ally."*

Tabba nodded his direction in affirmation. The look in his eyes showed not just his pride in his two sons, I could also see and perceive the deep love my man carried for his sons. My heart overflowed with pride. I thought of my third son, Samuel…I missed him terribly.

This success of our people produced, as it often does, envy. Those in positions of political power desired, lusted after, and coveted what we had worked for generations to attain. We, as a people, would not allow history to repeat itself. We spent an entire day wandering among the unending acres of orchards and fields. I greeted the workers, those gifted in working with the dust of Mother Earth. These were such special people, Apache, Comanche tending the land side by side. Families lived along the fields in our traditional teepee lodges. They were well paid but performed their work not due to the wealth their hands created, but due to the gifting they possessed. The gift of growing, creating life, and their deep love of Mother Earth. These people were doubly blessed.

And I loved them.

Our hearts were full of all we had seen in our journey across our Homeland. We were a nation, rich and powerful in all ways. Despite this fact, the *old ways* remained intact. Our schools instructed our young people from an ancient scroll, a complete manual of the *old ways*. *The People* were trained and capable of living our lives without any modern conveniences. Many of our people preferred such and lived in teepee lodges scattered across our Homeland. They hunted, gathered, and existed in the way we, as a people, had for centuries, and they were free to do so.

That evening the rovers transported us to the Ross home along the banks of the San Saba. It had taken us nine days to cross our reservation on horseback. The flight time in the rover was a mere seven minutes. I stared out the window as the aircraft accelerated through the sound barrier. My heart should have been full, but something in my spirit was troubled.

As I gazed out the small window at the blur along the surface of Mother Earth…I saw fire dancing among the buffalo herds below us. I had no ability to comprehend what the vision

These Thousand Days

could possibly mean, nor had I seen what our enemies would attempt this very day.

*****

The council would meet tonight. The autumn buffalo hunt would begin in just a few days. *The People* were gathering for the celebration and feast.

After a long hot soaking bath, my heart filled as I descended the elegant stairway into the great room. I watched my four grandchildren playing at the feet of my beautiful daughter, Little Abigail.

My only daughter, Little Abigail, possessed the kindest, gentlest spirit of any person I had ever met. As a child, she was so soft spoken and reserved we were concerned as parents whether she would ever emerge from the quiet calm shell she chose to live in. She never did, and eventually I was glad for her. Little Abigail's sincere heart desired an uncomplicated, simple life of becoming a mother, raising her children, and tending to the needs of others. She loved to read and cook, spending her days in quiet reserve. In retrospect, she was very much like her grandmother Abigail Ross. My daughter was simply a giver, and I loved her so for who she was as a mother and woman. She represented the very best of who we had become as a people.

"Are you rested now, Mother," Abigail said as she greeted me with a warm hug. Her expression changed abruptly at the sound of the warning siren. Why had I not seen this? I wondered, as the explosion shook the foundations of the massive home.

We gathered the children and walked calmly to the hidden stairwell. Once the children were settled within the safe room, I moved to my desk in the communication center. My computer monitor flashed a glowing red emergency code. I clicked specified icons and the face of my son William appeared. He sat calmly upon his war pony, the look on his face fierce and unwavering.

"They have attempted to breech the front gate, Mother. I have already given the order. The People are moving into the safety of the cavern system. Do not leave the bunker, Mother. This looks very serious. This is not a drill. Hundreds of troops stand at our gates."

Just then my phone vibrated. I left the video feed to William running on the computer display as I answered the call.

"Topusana, this is the president." The president of the United States of America identified himself, and within seconds, our system authenticated the feed. "I will ask this question for a final time…as I have warned you. The lives of your people will depend on your answer. Will you surrender the refinery and power plant now? I will give you five minutes to consider your answer."

I looked at the expression on the face of my son William as he motioned to his fellow Warriors to begin the targeting and counterattack. Within seconds, the hundreds of UN troops who gathered outside our gates met their death. They simply fell dead in their tracks. Those manning weapons or vehicles slumped lifeless in their firing stations and driver's seats.

The weapon worked. We were never certain it would; we had no way of testing it without revealing its presence to our enemies.

I looked again to my son for confirmation. He spoke in our native tongue. *"Operation Wolf is a success."*

"Mr. President, I do not need five minutes. Your army is dead."

I ended the call.

Chapter 8

The Year 2070

My first two sons were born in the year 2020. I never imagined twin brothers could be so unique and different, even exact opposites. William was a Warrior. He was so much like his father, Tabba, fierce, independent, and skilled in the *old ways*. He had been trained from childhood by both his father, Tabbananica, and his grandfather Tenahpu. His giftings and abilities were beyond compare. William was one of our most gifted hunters and extremely skilled as a tracker. His talents and insights were obviously a gift, and he used those giftings with an intentional purpose. William was a natural born defender, protector Warrior, like his grandfather, my father, Tenahpu.

William had attended West Point and graduated at the top of his class. In war college he also excelled. During that time, we maintained friendly negotiations and a healthy relationship with contacts in the United States government. Much changed in the years following his training. Over time it became clear to William he was being used. Those generals and commanders in positions of power needed and secretly sought out information from William concerning our Homeland. They desired what only we possessed. His counterintelligence work on behalf of our nation was invaluable. We knew precisely who our enemies were and what they were planning.

David, William's twin brother, was very much the opposite, quite withdrawn and studious. He spent his days reading the great philosophers, world religions, science journals, and the histories of nations. David was a brilliant scholar. Harvard law was "mind numbing and dull," as he would say. His time spent in Israel working with the world's leading scientists filled his brilliance with purpose.

Israel is where "Wolf" had been conceived and born. Tenahpu had a longtime friend and contact by the name of Abram Levi. With Abram's assistance, David gained access to Israeli intelligence and warfare development. His research was a breakthrough in technology and warfare. If what he had conceived proved to be possible…never again would men wage war in the traditional way with ships, tanks, aircraft, bombs, and bullets.

David Nica's creation had been tested and proven this very day. We were now the smallest, most powerful nation on Earth. Our enemies had no idea how powerful we had just become. Wolf, we would soon discover, had proved to be incredibly accurate and deadly. The EMP (electromagnetic pulse) targeted only the frequency band of the human heart. David had assured me that even the birds and small game would not be affected upon its release. This also proved to be true as we would discover in the days that followed. The test: animals were healthy and very much alive, all of them.

This day, individuals in positions of power would begin to fear us, for very good reason.

Some of our enemies surely knew how willing my Warrior

son William Nica was to use our newfound military might at the slightest threat to our Homeland.

*****

"Mother, are you there?" William transmitted.

"Yes, William, I am here. We are all safe."

"I have just ordered the decontamination of the bodies. The drone helicopters are on scene. Twenty-four hours is required."

"I understand; we will stay put. I will rendezvous with The People *at the north camp. The hunt will proceed as scheduled."*

"I will join you in council tonight, Mother. Have you heard from Samuel?"

I paused a moment, lost in thought. *"Nothing yet, William, should we risk a transmission?"*

"Yes. It is time," he replied.

"I'll look forward to seeing you, son. Thank you for what you have done for The People *this day."*

The screen faded to a blank grey for a moment, then the screensaver painting of me and Prairie Song filled the computer display. I breathed deeply, longing for and remembering our intimate embrace.

In that moment, I sensed something deep in my spirit from across the earth concerning my third son, Samuel. My youngest son was born to us five years after the twins. I felt we had somehow lost him. Although he was extremely successful in his career as a Navy pilot, airline captain, and other distinguished pursuits, he had left our world on the reservation. He was drawn to something out there in the white man's world that we could not provide. I understood on some level a man's need to succeed and to become something or make something of himself. However, in my gift of visions I knew my youngest son, Samuel Nica, or Kicking Fox, as his grandfather named him, would have a much deeper purpose and calling on his life.

Kicking Fox was a true Warrior at heart. How long would it be before his warrior spirit truly awakened and he fulfilled his life's calling? I was indeed beginning to feel a stirring from the Great Spirit concerning my third born son.

Chapter 9

The Year 2070

The cave fires burned brightly that night. I gazed into every face within the sacred circle. My love for my family and my people overflowed from my heart as Tosahwi began the ancient songs. We sang as one, lifting our praise to the heavens. My sons and daughter worshipped in spirit and truth alongside the other council members. Hantaywee (Faithful One) recited the prayers to our Creator. I could sense and feel the presence of the Spirit. I was humbled that the Creator would bless us with His presence.

The council agreed: tomorrow the bodies would be removed and buried in a mass grave. The grave had already been dug. At first light our equipment would load and move them far from here; it was the most hygienic thing to do. Our latest security report confirmed all armies had been vaccinated. But we would not be misled. I would make certain our people were safe. Germ warfare had been used against our people in the distant past. I would never forget how smallpox had eliminated many of our people…in another time.

"Has Topusana seen the future concerning repercussions from these deaths?" Tosahwi questioned.

"*I have*," I replied. I struggled to explain what I had seen and comprehended this very day. I paused. Conversation was never to be rushed in council. The men and women within the sacred circle nodded in agreement. The pipe was passed. We smoked and listened as the fire crackled. After a quiet pause I stood. *"The United States has no other troops to send. They have paid this army to arrive at our gates with dollars that are worthless. The United Nations will surely withdraw any remaining soldiers at the death of so many. They have no will to fight. I have seen…they have no courage."*

The news was met with affirmation in the form of nods and grunts. My son William, our protector Warrior, rose to speak next.

*"*Wolf *is being recharged as we speak; the weapon will be usable again in a few short hours. For the present time, we must signal our people to stay underground and hidden. My contacts in Israel are certain there are no remaining satellites that are operable. Still, it would be wise to assume otherwise and stay hidden."*

The council agreed and the signals were sent along our underground communication system.

We would delay the buffalo hunt by one day. I was excited yet apprehensive. The hunt was my favorite time of year. Our entire tribe lived in the *old ways* for one full moon. We followed the buffalo herds, hunting and processing every usable part of these glorious animals. We feasted nightly, shared the tales from old around our sacred fires. We sang the ancient songs as we traveled across our homelands. For one full month we would live wild and free. I treasured this remarkable time of blessed traditional native life.

I moved to my sleeping room within the cavern, and I thought of my adoptive mother Abigail Ross. I wondered how long it might be before she returned from the *Dream Time*. It could be years, I thought, or they might possibly return tomorrow. I missed her deeply. As I lay in the comfort of the soft cool sand, I whispered a prayer for her safety and quick return.

Sleep came to me quickly. My dreams were once again filled with visions and memories of a different time and place, a time when we did not practice the *old ways* for only one month but lived them out our entire lives. I longed for that time again. Life was much simpler in that time.

Although, it was a time of extreme danger.

In my dreams that night I saw again my third son. Samuel sat by his fire on the edge of the Outback half a world away. His songs came to me, and I sang along with him…the song of war. I clearly saw the Warrior heart that had awakened. Knowledge and comfort rested within my soul at this revelation. My son Samuel, Kicking Fox, would now live the life he had been set apart and trained for. His Warrior spirit had finally awakened.

Chapter 10

Abigail Ross
The Year 1800

I loved the mornings most. But there was so much I loved about my time spent in this special place. The high mountains of New Mexico were spectacular in countless ways: the winter snow, the vistas overlooking the White Sands desert, the clear running streams of sweet cold water. My senses came alive in these early morning hours as I observed this beautiful land. I breathed the cool mountain air into my lungs as I stood outside the entrance of the hidden cavern. Tenahpu, my husband, or Daklugie as he was known here among the Apache, took my hand as we began our descent along the ancient trail.

We had come here at my suggestion. Although it may have been a dangerous decision to enter the *Dream Time,* I wanted to see and know and experience just how, where, and what life was really like for my friends, my daughter Sana, and my new husband, Tenahpu. I admit I also desired the benefits of the *Dream Time* travel. It was plainly obvious the aging process was slowed considerably for those who had traveled along its mysterious course.

We were, in terms of Earth years, very old now, nearly one hundred. But both Dak and I looked to be in our sixties, maybe younger. Our bodies were sound, and we were both in excellent physical condition. I felt much like a twenty-year-old on the inside. Dak likewise, was strong and virile. He remained handsome with shiny black hair and chiseled rugged features. His eyes remained that piercing smoky gray that reflected his intensity. This morning we had again made love in the little sleeping room within the cavern, passionate, earth-shattering, deeply satisfying love. My life as the woman of Daklugie was filled with pleasures I had never imagined.

This day we would travel the ancient trail, descending along its path. We needed fresh meat. The mountain sheep Daklugie had killed two weeks ago was almost gone. I had gained a taste for antelope in our travel across the plains. We would move out of the high mountains and onto the rolling hills and plains east of the mountains for the hunt.

The walk invigorated me. It was now late summer; Dak estimated the year to be around 1800. In this time in which we now walked, the air is what I noticed most. It was fresher, cleaner, and it even tasted good. I never noticed that in the previous time in which I had lived. Air did not seem to have any taste; if I noticed air in my past time, it was when it had been fouled by a diesel truck or an oil platform. I breathed deeply, filling my lungs with pure oxygen. I gazed at my man as he led the way along the trail, handsome, athletic, and filled with knowledge and skills that would provide all we needed to live and exist in this pristine wilderness.

****

These Thousand Days

I caught the scarcely perceptible motion of his hand—the sign of warning. I froze. What had he seen? Dak, dressed in his skins, blended into the landscape, and disappeared. I attempted the same. But they had seen me.

My heartbeat rose; I could feel its beating pulse in my neck and temples. I attempted to breath as quietly as possible. But I heard the movement from behind me. They came as one.

From the corner of my vision, I saw the war club raised, and then the fierce eyes of an enemy bore through me. An arrow from my man's bow penetrated the warrior's chest as he fell away from me. I ran toward Dak, calling out in fear. In an instant I knew and felt and understood what my friends and family had escaped.

Terror.

I knew what it was to be hunted. I felt the horror. I experienced the fear they must have all felt. Still, I ran, driven by a deep burning fear.

I saw a little divide in the earth ahead of me. Yes, I might make it…my feet dug into the soft earth. Just two or three strides remained. Time slowed, as if I were moving in slow motion. I saw from above how my feet dug into the soil. A trail of dust and sand rose into the air behind each stride. My arms strained in perfect motion and timing with each stride. I could feel the veins in my neck bulging at the effort. My soft golden hair flew wild behind my movement.

I saw from an odd perspective above and to the side of my escape route…the fear on my face and in my eyes. I leapt into the small arroyo. I sailed through the air; I flew across the exposed chasm that separated me from exposure to the relative safety of the arroyo. I landed hard. I heard the gruesome sound of my leg breaking. I rolled against the side of the dirt embankment. Pain shot through my body. I attempted to rise; the searing pain stopped my movement. My vision blurred, the light faded from the sky, then there was nothing.

Chapter 11

Abigail Ross
The Year 1800

I awakened to the sound of drums. A woman stood over me, peering curiously into my eyes. She offered me a drink from a gourd filled with water. I accepted. As my senses came alive, I became aware of my thirst. My mouth and throat were extremely dry; my lips were cracked and bleeding. The cool water offered instant relief as I swallowed. Becoming further aware, the pain in my leg came alive, sharp and intense. I sat up. The woman pointed at my leg and made the sign of breaking. I nodded and spied the make-do splint that had been fashioned and tied around my lower leg. I took in the scene before me: a hastily set up camp, a dozen or so Warriors with painted faces. They spoke in a language I had never heard. I knew these were enemies. I realized my hands were bound. A man noticed I had awakened. The woman moved away from me and disappeared.

The man moved in my direction. He grabbed my hair, then tore my skins away from my chest. He pushed me into the dust.

I felt, more than heard the earth sing to me. A gift to my soul…an intended distraction as the man entered me violently.

Again, my perspective shifted to slightly above the scene, and I saw the next man lay upon my broken body…and the next.

I thought of Prairie Song. I knew her terror. I now understood her death.

The earth hummed its tune of peace in the distant recesses of my soul. The darkness overtook me again. I welcomed its presence and drifted far away from the reality of violation.

****

Late into the dark night I awakened to the sound of the night bird calling. Daklugie!

A rifle shot rang out, echoing through the night. Then another shot, and another. I lost count. Within minutes they were all dead. He came to me, lifting me gently. He carried me away from this place. In his arms, my heart spilled tears of relief. I faded away again only to awaken hours later. He carried me away from the pain, away from the violation. I melted into his strong arms. Miles must have passed in the night; when I awakened again, I was lying in his arms. I was far from what had happened, far from the nightmare and close to my man. It was all that mattered. I was safe in his arms. I had no idea how broken and wounded my body and my soul were.

The fire glowed, dimly projecting waves of dancing light upon the art drawings on the cavern wall. He stood, then moved toward me. Kneeling at my side, he examined the splint and bandages on my leg. He touched my face and hair with a gentle hand. "We should return home soon, Abby."

I reached for him. I cannot explain the level of deep desire I felt for him. I was wounded, damaged, a broken vessel. But I wanted him to have me. To be a part of me. To assure me that I still held value…perhaps my soul needed to know…that I was still desirable to him.

He kissed me gently on the cheek. "Soon, Abby, not now, but soon. I am so sorry my love…that I failed you." He turned and moved away from me.

"You have protected all of us, for years now. You saved me. They would have killed me. You know that is true." I spoke through the tears I could not hold. "You are my everything… and I do not want to go back. I want to know more."

He looked at me with an understanding in his countenance. "You may need medical attention I cannot give you in this place. We can be home in a day. Are you certain, Abby?"

"If we leave now, this is all I will ever think about and remember. I need to recover right here. I need to live out the good days ahead. Show me your world, Dak. Show me the goodness of your people."

He breathed deeply. "Yes, I see and understand." He turned and began again his drawing upon the cavern wall.

I watched for days in fascination as the masterpiece slowly revealed his own pain. The art revealed what lay beneath. The paintings revealed what is for most men…always unseen. His heart, his soul, his mind. I knew from what I observed…I still had value and he desired me in every way.

Chapter 12

Abigail Ross
The year 1800

The days slipped by like a gentle wind nearly indiscernible as it ripples across a calm lake. Late summer turned to fall quickly in the high mountains. The nights were cold. The aspen leaves turned a golden hue that shimmered and sang in the autumn sun, and I began to heal.

We had traveled alone from Texas across the plains. Dak, through a series of signs placed in strategic locations along the mountains, communicated with the Apache. In the days following the attack, we stayed hidden along the edges of what Dak referred to as the *ancient trail*. I was amazed that *The People* located and understood the signs Dak left for them. Within a week, an entire band of Apache set up winter camp along a bold flowing creek within a deep isolated canyon. We were well hidden and well supplied with fresh meat from the little ponds along the canyon floor that teamed with trout and the plentiful deer and elk that roamed the high mountains of New Mexico.

The women took me in and tended to my needs. *The People*, as a whole, were gifted in every possible way. Some were expert hunters. Others gifted in medicine and the knowledge of natural healing plants. Still others were gifted in song or prayer. My friend Bina (Music) possessed a special gifting. She could see into another person's heart. She could feel and relate to what another soul had endured in life. Bina had a kind, compassionate heart that ministered love, forgiveness, and healing to those who most needed it.

"Sky Eyes, (the name the women had given me due to my pale blue eyes) *we will walk the ancient trail today?"* Bina asked with a questioning look. My body was healing, although my leg as it knit remained somewhat bent from the break below my knee. It would remain so the rest of my days. This physical reminder of the attack and rape I had suffered would serve as a lifelong awareness and reminder of what evil men were capable. My heart would forever be knit with the granddaughter I had never met…Prairie Song…who had died at the hands of such evil men.

"Yes, I would love to walk with you today, Bina," I replied. We gathered our things, a water carrier, our long knives, and Bina took up her bow and quiver. We never encountered a circumstance requiring the weapons, but Bina knew having them brought a level of security to me. She knew exactly what was needed to begin the healing of my mind and soul. She began to sing the songs of creation as we walked along the ancient trail.

I treasured my walks with Bina.

"The men will make war on the tribe from the north soon?" I questioned as we rested in a small clearing.

"Dak has located the camp of the remaining warriors. This confrontation will not be a war, Sky Eyes. You must understand, Dak is a protector Warrior. Even though he killed the group of men that attacked you, he will not rest until their evil has been eliminated from the earth."

These Thousand Days

I breathed deeply and nodded toward Bina. I understood. It was a comfort on some level in my soul to know none of this group of men would survive. I also knew Dak would be safe, even in his pursuit of these men.

Dak and I were uncertain the weapons he had cached in the cavern on the San Saba would still be there once we traveled in *Dream Time*. Nor were we certain those weapons would be operable once we moved into the new time. Both questions had been answered soon after we had awakened and confirmed again on the day of the attack by the northern tribe. Dak was indeed a protector Warrior. He had been trained in a different time. His sniper rifle along with his skills were no match for the weapons the enemy Warriors carried, although they had been supplied with muskets by the Spaniards. More importantly, I saw in his eyes daily the fierceness and resolve that only blood would satisfy.

"How is your heart today, Sky Eyes?" Bina waited and listened patiently as she did every day. Today would be different…I told her everything that day upon the ancient trail, every detail. I let out all my pain and fear and wounding.

She listened for hours. Once I ended the emptying of my soul, she simply nodded in understanding. The aspen leaves performed their shimmering dance. The wind whispered in the blue trees. In the calm of His presence, the pain in my heart departed my soul and mind.

Bina began to sing.

****

Ten days later Dak returned to the camp in the hidden deep canyon. He carried his sniper rifle across his shoulders. I noticed immediately he carried only one ammunition belt. He had departed the camp with two. I breathed deeply, knowing their evil had been erased from the earth.

That night as we lay in our teepee lodge, the fire burned softly, the wolves sang their songs, and the stars danced across the backbone of the high mountains. For the first time in many moons, I gave myself again to my man. Dak was uncertain at first. I made sure he would never be so again. We became lost in ecstasy; our lives simultaneously healed in our oneness.

We were whole again.

As I lay in my man's arms, I could hear the songs of Bina, her tune carried along by the night wind throughout the camp.

I knew in my heart we could now return to our former life. I had seen enough. I understood completely what my daughter Topusana had endured. I also understood how my granddaughter Prairie Song had died. In the future, I would do all within my power to make certain this terrifying history would not repeat itself.

The *Dream Time*, in a few short days, would take us home.

Chapter 13

Abigail Ross
The year 1800

We traveled down and out of the high mountains toward the east and south. I was amazed again out how quickly the terrain changed from high alpine meadows above the tree line, to the southwest Sonoran Desert filled with a multitude of dangers. Every plant seemed capable of tearing flesh and each animal or insect equipped with deadly defenses or poisons. The travel was a struggle for me.

Dak knew the way by heart. He had navigated his way across this high desert numerous times. I know I slowed our progress. My ability to move quickly had been hindered by the break in my leg. He was, however, extremely patient with me and was slowly teaching me how to move with the land.

"*The People* move along ridgetops or game trails. There is always a path even in the most remote land. Find your way, Abby. Let the earth show you. Watch each step you take, yet see ahead," he said to me as we moved along an outcropping of boulders. I was beginning to understand. When we exited the boulder field, we could see for miles across a low plain. A river flowed in the distance at least twenty-five miles ahead of us.

"Where is the best route to the river, Abby?" he questioned as we gazed across the empty expanse of desert before us. Suddenly, I could see the way or feel it might have been more what my mind experienced. I took the lead. "Yes, that's it, Abby, follow in your mind in the way you have seen."

Dak was an excellent teacher. He was patient in a way I had never before experienced. I knew he was being gentle with me. That gentleness was a trait that would forever grace our relationship from this time forward. I loved him even more.

The following day we arrived along the banks of the river. Dak started a fire and caught several large fish by hand. He gathered water in containers as I prepared the fish. That evening we dined on the succulent flesh of fresh catfish and the crispy refreshing taste of grilled cattail root. The stars began to appear and display the grandeur of creation and the Creator. It would be the last day we would spend in this time. "I think it best we do not travel to the San Saba for the *Dream Time*, Abby." He looked in the direction of my leg. I understood. "There is a place we will be safe not far from here."

I nodded in agreement.

I opened my arms, welcoming my man. I knew he would take care of me and keep us safe. I felt the earth sing to me again that night…again comforting me as she had the night of the attack. This night was much different; two souls loved the night away beneath a starry canopy along the banks of a pristine river. We were free, natural, wild, and filled with the blessing of Creator. I never felt so loved.

The following morning, we moved several miles away from the river into a deep draw. The entrance to the cavern was large. Once inside the cavern, the massive rooms were like nothing I had ever seen. An entire other-worldly place appeared before us. Huge columns of formations from ceiling to floor reflected the dim light of Dak's torch. I was amazed at the wonder before us as we made our way along. "This is such an incredible, unbelievable place," I said. My voice returned to me in repeated fading echoes emanating from the darkness ahead. I was in awe.

Dak assisted me in the climb up a smooth surface and across a narrow rock bridge that led to a little hidden room. I peered out the little entrance to the room and saw the torch he had left burning on the cavern floor hundreds of yards away. The light from the torch reflected off the cavern ceiling that must have been at least two hundred feet above us. This place was simply majestic.

****

The sweet fragrance of the incense is what I remember most. Made from native flower blossoms and wild honey, the scent crisp and so distinct…it always sent my mind to the ceremony of *Dream Time*. We drank from the sacred bowl; the fire burned softly as I lay hand in hand with Dak. Our little room was well supplied with stored food and water. We were going home.

I remembered his last words as I drifted into the deep sleep of *Dream Time*.

"Carlsbad. That is what they will call this place in the future, Abby. Carlsbad."

Chapter 14

Abigail Ross
Present day
The year 2070

We awakened within minutes of one another. As my awareness came alive, I was frightened at what I heard and saw. Voices and light. They seemed out of place. They *were* out of place.

Dak moved groggily toward the little opening into our room. He stumbled as his vision adjusted to the light emanating from the cavern floor below. "What is it, Dak?" I questioned.

I also stood on shaky legs and moved toward the entrance. We both were stunned at the scene below. Groups of what appeared to be families or tourists moved along a well-lit path below. Their voices echoed throughout the gigantic room.

"I thought this might happen. We have obviously awakened in modern day, Abby. Although Tosahwi has perfected the estimated awakening time, we cannot really be sure of the exact date. This cave became a tourist attraction in the 1960s. From the looks of the clothing they are wearing, it must be later than that."

I looked over his shoulder and spotted a woman taking photos with a cell phone.

"Much later, Dak," I said, pointing at the women with the phone.

"Yes, I see, perhaps we are close to the time frame we departed." He moved away from the entrance and located his pack frame. While rummaging through its contents he withdrew his satellite phone, pushed the power button…and nothing happened.

"It has solar capabilities but obviously not within the cavern." We looked into one another's eyes and asked the question on both our minds simultaneously. "How do we get out?"

"One problem at a time," Dak said. "We need to eat and hydrate."

"I understand," I said as I moved to the supply of food we had stashed in our little room. I opened a skin filled with dried fruit and meat. We both ate sparingly. I quickly discovered our water carriers were empty. "We need water, Dak."

He looked over the opening again. They appeared to be moving on. He listened intently for a few moments. "Others are making their way down the trail. I'll go for water soon, Abby. I hope I have the strength to climb out and back up."

"Let's not risk it, Dak, let's just eat what we can and get out. We can drink from the streams on the way out."

"What about my rifle? How do we get past the guides or security? We aren't exactly dressed for the occasion either."

I looked at our clothing. We were dressed in beautifully decorated traditional animal skins and moccasins. Dak had his bow, long knife, a quiver of arrows, and a war club in addition to his sniper rifle.

"I have an idea, Abby. Let's climb down the formation. Just follow my lead if we are questioned."

These Thousand Days

"I'm so thirsty, Dak. Should we wait until they close for the day?"

Dak shouldered his sniper rifle and the soft deer skin daypack filled with dried meat. "We need water now. Waiting might be dangerous. I'm sorry, my love. I knew this might happen. I just couldn't imagine you walking to Texas with your leg. I will protect you. Are you with me?" he asked with a look of determination mixed with concern.

"Yes, husband. I don't suppose a tour guide is much of a concern when facing an Apache Warrior." We both smiled as he embraced me. His expression changed to one of fierceness.

"I will never allow another man to ever bring you harm, Abby. I will die before that happens." The intensity in his eyes spoke more than his words.

"I know that, my love. Let's go."

We waited a few moments at the opening to our little room where we had traveled along the backbone of time…over two hundred years.

Dak made it to the lighted trail below us without being spotted. I moved much slower. My body was just not recovered enough for the difficult descent. I heard the next group moving in our direction. Dak, after filling a water carrier and drinking deeply from the little lake, calmly removed his sat phone from the pack and began acting as if he were taking pictures of me. I struggled fifty feet above him, slowly making my way down the smooth steep slope. A voice called out from below.

"You, there! You're not supposed to leave the trail." The voice was loud and commanding. Dak moved toward the man.

"It's just a photo op," he explained while faking his snapping away of pictures. "Have you seen the rest of the Indian actors? We seemed to have gotten separated from the group."

The park ranger reached for his radio. "I'll have to check this out. I don't recall anything on the agenda today."

Dak grasped the radio hand of the ranger and spoke something I could not hear. I continued down the difficult slope. I reached the bottom and stepped across the chain fencing onto the trail just as the man backed away from Dak with an alarmed look on his face.

"Get a photo of us…look at his face, Abby, just what we were hoping for. The white man startled by the Indians in the cavern."

"You two are nuts. Give me my radio back, sir. Now!" the ranger demanded. A group of tourists began to back away, uncertain where this was going.

"Ah, come on, just a couple more pictures, please," Dak said. The ranger reached for the radio in Dak's hand. Dak instantly threw the radio into the small lake adjacent to the trail.

"Did you get that, Abby?"

The man turned toward me as I made the motion of snapping a photo, although, I did not have a camera.

We turned and ran in the direction of the entrance. The park ranger froze as we made our escape. He had no way to communicate with others. He called after us, "Stop, hey, come back here."

We moved rapidly up the paved trail and exited the cavern into a pouring rain. A number of tourists pointed at us as we crossed the large parking lot. We paused a moment behind a parked bus, then walked casually into the desert. After a half mile of travel, Dak stopped again and observed our back trail. The rain increased in intensity. The thunder rolled along the low hills. Lightning danced across the afternoon sky.

"No one followed us, Abby."

I drank deeply from the water carrier. The smells of fresh rain and the amazing scents of a flowering desert met my senses as we turned and walked away from Carlsbad Caverns National Park.

We were on our way home.

****

Two days later the sun finally showed itself from behind the parting cloud cover. The satellite phone, after being exposed to the sunlight for a while, indicated a two percent charge. We had made a camp beside a small flowing stream. We had eaten well on fresh rabbit Dak had taken in his snares. The pure clean water from the stream strengthened our bodies. We had recovered from the *Dream Time*. The distance to reach our homeland was over five hundred miles, a daunting task to cross on foot.

Dak held the little satellite phone in the direction of the sunlight and hit the dial button. To our surprise a familiar voice answered on the second ring.

"Grandfather? Is that really you?" William Nica's voice echoed loud and clear on the speaker.

"Yes, William, we have returned. We are safe." The sound of loud explosions filled the air emanating from the little speaker. Then the call ended, and the signal bars disappeared.

Dak and I looked into one another's eyes. "I'm not sure what just happened, Abby. That did not sound good. I'm not sure we have many options."

I began to pack our meager belongings into the little pack skin. Dak filled the water carrier and within ten minutes we were walking east. Traveling at my lead, not upon the land, but with the land.

"Find the best path, Abby. Listen to Mother Earth as you move. She will show you the best way."

I understood. The earth began her silent song as we traveled along in the way of *The People*. I hummed in time with the tune…One step at a time my child. One step at a time. I heard her voice whisper in my heart.

Chapter 15

Topusana
Present day
The Year 2070

The first campsite was chosen by Tabba after a walk of twenty-five miles. With excitement and eagerness, *The People* took to the task of setting up the teepees and starting the lodge fires. The smell of roasting buffalo meat wafted throughout the camp. Songs sung among the family groups drifted joyfully in the air. My heart was filled at the sights and scenes being lived out before me. My people had survived. Not only survived, but my people were thriving.

I took a deep breath and whispered a prayer for my mother Abby. Perhaps she and my father Tenahpu would arrive soon. I walked along the makeshift path between the tepee lodges toward the council lodge. Smoke was already rising from the smoke hole. The elders were gathering near the council lodge, awaiting my arrival. I greeted family members and friends as I moved along. *The People* were happy. That was all that mattered in this moment.

****

Early the next morning, the sun rested on the eastern horizon, the sky aglow in radiant tints of reds, oranges, and exploding pink hues. The camp was awakening. So many days we had lived in this way. This *Old Way*. The earth welcomed our presence and our activities. Today would be the first full hunting day. I wandered to the edge of the camp amidst the growing activities and preparations. I paused as I did each morning and again whispered a prayer for my mother Abby.

Tabba, along with several Warriors, departed the camp toward the north with a high wave of his lance. Even from this distance, I saw the excitement on his face. It would only be a few hours before they returned. I seated myself in the buffalo grass, closed my eyes, and soaked in the goodness of Mother Earth. Breathing in deeply, I began my worship. One hour later…I saw.

My mind could not grasp what I had seen. My body shook; my heart raced. I stood and ran toward the camp, calling out my war cry. Would we have enough time?

****

Within the sacred lodge, I shared the vision with the elders. Thousands of troops were moving toward us at this very moment. *"They will arrive from the west. That is all I have seen."*

"Send the scout Warriors now!" Tosahwi spoke. All nodded in agreement. Within minutes the scouts departed on horseback. They would travel to the west and report back before the sun set.

"William left with the first group of hunters at daylight. Send runners with the news we need him desperately." I had the ability to use the sat phone, but we knew any electronic communication would be intercepted. Again, the group was

all in agreement we would communicate in the old way. A second detachment departed to the north within minutes of the order.

"*And* The People?" Tosahwi questioned.

"*Have them prepare for war,*" I said. "*The Bands from the south should arrive by afternoon. However, we should send runners to the south also. They can warn them in advance.*"

"*What else might we do, Topusana?*" the elders questioned.

"*Send the women and children…all our young boys and young girls to the cavern.*" The order was met with a silence. My intention was clear. This had forever been our emergency plan. This order was to assure the survival of our people…in the event the worst happened. In the event we were decimated by the army from across the sea I had seen in my vision.

****

William, along with his father, Tabba, and the other Warriors raced their war ponies across the prairie. The men had seen the attack coming. The buffalo had warned them.

The stalk was progressing smoothly. They moved silently through the underbrush downwind from the herd. Tabba knew it was not possible the buffalo had detected them. Then the animals stampeded without warning. William rose from his hidden location as the buffalo fled. He spotted the massive formation of men moving through the sparse cover of brush. There were too many. He would need to deploy Wolf.

The first explosion was well behind the fleeing Warriors. William knew the next volley of explosives would be much closer. They separated when seeing the hand signals from Tabbananica. Their ponies were the swiftest on Earth. But could they avoid the targeting system being deployed? William changed course. The next explosion rang in his ears, so he changed course again, his fellow Warriors doing the same. For now, the tactic worked. The emergency code on his sat phone sounded. There were two specific people who had the ability to communicate with him during the annual hunt: his mother, Topusana, and his grandfather Tenahpu.

William drove his horse into a low arroyo. He momentarily came to a stop and looked at the display in disbelief. *"Grandfather? Is that really you?"* The explosion buffeted the air with a percussion that knocked William from his mount. The sat phone flew out of his hand. His war pony would not rise from the sandy bottom of the arroyo. The horse lay pawing the ground in a growing pool of blood…then moved no more.

William retrieved the phone and ran. With his feet digging deeply into the sand, he strained to gain traction. He saw the little depression within the bank of the arroyo. He paused, then smoothed the ground, erasing his tracks as he moved; he quickly climbed into the little cave along the side of the arroyo and hid himself in the darkness. Within minutes, he could hear the soldiers advancing toward him, speaking a strange language.

Mandarin? He thought to himself. He knew he was correct in his interpretation of the language. The Chinese were advancing across his Homeland? If true, he was not that surprised. The United States military had focused primarily on philosophy and political correctness over the last two decades. They were in no fashion equipped militarily to win a war, much less an invasion. The possibilities raced through his mind. Had the United States been invaded and defeated in less than a day? Or was there something more sinister at play here?

The sat phone beeped softly as William quickly silenced the device. He sent the correct code successfully. Surely his mother and Grandfather received the code. "Deploy Wolf! North and west. Red Army!" William punched in the coordinates of his present position and noted to center the attack there. He prayed they would deploy the weapon despite him being within the field of fire.

He sent another message. "Deploy Wolf! Immediately!" He began to dig.

Perhaps he could get deep enough. Ten feet of earth was needed. He thought the arroyo was seven or eight feet deep. Perhaps if he dug in just a couple of feet. The sand floor was soft as he rapidly worked, losing several fingernails in the desperate process. The little depression deepened quickly. William took his bow and began scraping the roof of the little cavern. The roof collapsed in front of him, slightly filling in the entrance. He turned and again began to dig out the remaining space that surrounded him. After a few moments he settled within the two-foot-deep depression he had scraped out and began to cover himself with the loose sand from the cave-in. Once again, he reached for the sat phone and programmed his location. He would not press the send button for at least one hour. In the darkness of the arroyo, encased within Mother Earth, William prayed with all his heart. His prayers, he thought, were always heard. He was not certain how the prayers of a Warrior pleading for the destruction of thousands of souls might be answered.

His faith was strong.

One hour later he began to dig his way out. William analyzed the possibilities. He had either dug deep enough to survive or the tribe had not deployed Wolf. He prayed even more fervently as he dug, hoping that the former was the case. Wolf had the ability to target thousands. He prayed his father and the other Warriors had outrun the invaders. They needed two miles. He calculated the times of the call, the speed of the horses, and distances required. It would be possible. The calculations were too close to determine the outcome.

Two hours later, William stood outside his little cave, observing the unimaginable scene before him. He pressed the send button on his sat phone, indicating his present position. He knew he was only a half day's walk back to camp. Maybe only a couple of hours if he ran.

He set out at an easy jog on a direct course to the camp. The bodies were scattered across the prairie in a formation he had seen many times. These armies were often displayed on media clips marching in perfect unison—the video footage often broadcast to the world as a sign of military might. William thought how foolish it was to deploy this tactic in an actual military campaign. This formation march must have made easy calculations for Wolf to target the enormous number of troops in such a small area. He estimated five thousand men had died within a mile of his hidden location. As he continued his jog to the camp, it occurred to him the enemy would never advance from just one direction.

The Art of War was still taught to most military commanders in the Far East. He stopped suddenly and typed the next message quickly. "Check all flanks; there ARE more troops."

Why were they not responding?

Chapter 16

Topusana
The year 2070

Topusana and the others in the sacred circle paused at the sound of her sat phone pinging. She read the message and gave the order without hesitation. "Deploy Wolf north and west," she typed into the sat phone, forwarding the coordinates sent by William to the command center in the basement of the Ross home. David received the message and began the targeting sequence that identified within seconds 5,420 individual heartbeats. David, seeing the data, prayed one of those heartbeats was not that of his twin brother, William. He double checked the data and understood…William was in fact within the field of fire. David had no choice…he pressed the deploy button.

Sana began her prayers as her tears fell upon the sacred buffalo robe she was seated upon. The elders joined in her prayer with the holy songs of the past.

Two hours later Sana's sat phone pinged again. The message from William brought an answer to their prayers. He had somehow survived. The additional information was invaluable; there was certain to be a flanking movement from the enemy.

Sana, at risk of giving their position away, first ordered the entire camp to move to the large cavern. Word traveled quickly throughout the camp; within minutes *The People* were moving. Sana then dialed the number for David in the command center. *"Mother, I have a location on William."* David spoke in a code he hoped the enemy could not decipher. Alternating every other word first in Comanche then the next in Apache. Sana mimicked his speech code.

"I understand, David. We will send Warriors to his location. William is certain there is another flanking movement. I have seen nothing in my visions. Scan the entire homeland."

"I understand, Mother. They will be southwest or northeast. Never in opposite directions. They have intercepted your transmission. Even though they may not understand, you must move The People *now!"*

"The order has been given; we are moving to the large cavern." Sana ended the call at the sound of a large explosion.

The People were already one quarter of a mile away from the enemy targeting and within another three or four minutes safely out of range of the exploding ordinance bombarding the deserted camp. Although several members were injured in the first blast, there were no fatalities.

David began the scan in two directions only…it would save precious time. Knowing *The Art of War* himself proved invaluable.

****

Tabbananica raced his war pony across the prairie in the direction of his son William. He let loose the tethered war pony that would provide a mount for William, knowing the horse would follow closely. William's pony moved alongside Tabba as they ran, panting wildly. Tabba smiled inwardly despite the situation. These were the finest war ponies on Earth…and the animals were relishing in the freedom and wildness of what they were bred to do as they sped across the open prairie.

****

Topusana's sat phone pinged again. She read the brief message, *"Wolf has been deployed north and east, Mother. Twenty-three thousand targets eliminated."*

What had these enemies attempted this day?

Chapter 17

Abigail Ross
The year 2070

With caution Dak and I approached the small former oil town under the cover of darkness. The high overcast allowed no moonlight or even starlight to penetrate its light-dampening veil. We had traveled for three full days now. Dak understood it was a risk to enter the town, but he had an idea of a safe place where we might communicate our location and the news of our arrival.

Dimly glowing lights shone here and there in the small town square, indicating there were still limited hours of the power grid operating here. We held to the back alleys and dark shadows as we approached the rear of the abandoned shop. Dak pried the rear door open, and we entered the building that had evidently been empty for years. Dak recalled that lasting memory when he so desperately needed a friend.

"It's still here!" Dak said in amazement. He flipped some switches as a dull hum emitted from the shortwave radio. In the glow of the faded dials on the face of the radio, Dak transmitted a message across the heavens. The signal bounced off the atmosphere and the earth numerous times as the call made its way halfway round the world.

"Abram, we have arrived. We can be found in the place you and I first met."

In a small apartment on the shores of the sea of Galilee, Abram Levi received the message loud and clear. Dak stood in front of the radio, fine-tuning the band frequency and listening intently at what he thought was an answer. "Did you hear that, Abby?"

"I think it sounded like, well, like just static." But Dak was convinced he had heard the voice of Abram…if for just a moment.

"What do we do now, Dak?"

"Now we wait, Abby; they will come for us."

****

Three hours later the rover departed the small oil town on the plains of eastern New Mexico. The pilot and two passengers disappeared into the night sky. Fifty thousand false tracks were generated by the cloaking and cloning technology. The destination along the banks of the San Saba would never be discovered. The rover departed the San Saba just ten minutes later, showing another one-hundred-fifty thousand cloned tracks upon its departure.

One hour later Tenahpu (The Man) and his woman Abigail Ross (Sky Eyes) entered the edges of the sacred fire. Tabba stood and greeted his father-in-law, his woman, Topusana, rose and moved to her mother, wrapping her arms around Abby in a loving, protecting embrace.

Chapter 18

Topusana
The Year 2070

One week later I sat in silence. The negotiations were going well. Our delegation consisted of myself, my sons William and David, along with my mother Abigail Ross, and Daklugie/Tenahpu the Warrior. The president of the United States along with his aids and military advisors sat on the opposite side of the table. Also in attendance was a delegation from China, including the president of the Chinese Communist Party.

The document contained language that translated words from Comanche to Mandarin to English, which was not an exact, literal, or clear communication. However, the leaders from all three countries understood the look of fierce resolve from both Warriors present, my son William, and his grandfather Daklugie/Tenahpu.

"Reparations are in order yet again, gentlemen," I said. The president lowered his eyes to the floor. "However, we wish to simply be left alone. And understand me clearly. *Wolf* will never be surrendered." I noted instantly the defiance in the countenance of the two men. I nodded toward David. The order would be implemented. He began to record the distinct heartbeat patterns of the two men. The words came to me from the Book of Truth and I spoke them aloud.

"For in the day of trouble He will keep me safe in His dwelling; He will hide me in His sacred tent and set me high upon a Rock. Then my head will be exalted above the enemies who surround me; at His sacred tent I will sacrifice with shouts of joy; I will sing and make music to the Lord."

The representatives from Israel that had coordinated the ceasefire and peace negotiations tapped away at their keyboards, evaluating every spoken word. At my words, I saw they paused in worship. The room fell silent for a hushed moment at the speaking of Truth.

"Here is my plan for reparations…I want you to hear the story of how the last peace negotiations unfolded for the Chief of my tribe."

The two leaders nodded in agreement.

"His name was Maguara. He was a faithful man who truly wished for a peace that never came to his life or his people. Sometimes over the course of time, we tend to forget what others have endured. However, *The People* will never forget. I will never forget."

And with that, I began the story of the Council House peace delegation. The story of women and children dying in the streets of San Antonio, Texas. The president of the United States listened intently, as did the leader of the Chinese Communist Party. It was obvious neither man knew our story.

David sat in silence while recording the distinct heartbeat patterns of the two men. His small hidden device silently, efficiently, and precisely targeted the pattern of each man's heartbeat. Upon our return to our Homeland, David would load the data into the weapon system Wolf.

Chapter 19

Topusana
The Following Night
My Dreams from the Year 1840

In the year 1840 along the banks of the San Saba, we walked hand in hand. It was springtime, the trees showing the bright pale green of early buds. The river gurgled along its course, clear and clean. I was troubled. Maguara and his procession had not been heard from since departing for the peace conference in San Antonio with the leaders of Texas.

Tabba became aware of the movement first. It was just a flash of something out of place. In the brush cover along the edge of the river, we inched closer. Then the songs met our ears. They came to us gently, a soft humming mingled in harmony with the light breeze and burbling of the river. Kota (Friend to Everyone), wife of Maguara, sat along the edge of the San Saba just a half mile below the camp. She was singing the songs of mourning.

We entered her presence quietly and sat alongside her. I joined in the songs, singing softly, as did Tabba. After an hour of worship had passed, Kota ended her songs and looked into my eyes. *"They killed most of our People, Sana."*

"I understand, Kota. There are others who escaped?"

"We numbered sixty, those who entered the Council House. Only eight women and children escaped. Fifty-two have passed due to the bullets of the Texans. Women, children, Warriors, and our Chief Maguara, my husband. They now walk with the Great Spirit. Theirs was a good death."

I moved to Kota and embraced her. She seemed to melt into my arms; I felt the surrender of her spirit. I knew this beautiful woman, this treasure of wisdom and understanding, would soon walk with her husband. I would do all within my power to guard and watch over her last days.

As we moved toward the Home Camp, Tabba peered into my eyes, a fierceness showing on his face. I knew he was in wonder that my vision was again correct. What I had seen in my conversation with Maguara as we moved across the frozen prairie had come to pass.

The hope that Chief Maguara held…had indeed cost many lives.

****

In my dreams, the lodge fire burned bright that night as we sat in the council circle. The news of the deaths of the members of the peace delegation brought a sobering reality to all. For the first time, the elders and Warriors alike were in complete agreement with what I had been saying for over two years. We must escape. Preparations would begin in earnest. I stared into the flames of the sacred fire. I spoke nothing that night.

I wondered how many would survive the next few seasons as we began our preparations. We had lost half of our Band at the Council House massacre. Would our remaining people survive? Tosahwi spoke what was in my heart and mind. *"Shall we all perish at the hands of the whites?"* His question was answered resoundingly this troubled night. We would escape into the *Dream Time*.

****

Topusana
The Year 2070

I awakened early the following morning. I lit a small candle and sat in wonder at the clarity of my dream. I again lingered within the memory of what had taken place so long ago. In retaliation, our Warriors led by my grandfather Buffalo Hump had dealt a tremendous blow to the Texans during the Great Raid. The attack and cost to the Texans would be studied and written about for centuries.

I thought of Kota. Her name, Friend to Everyone, was so true to the heart of who she was. I corrected myself, even though she had departed this world, I had met her in another time and place. I knew she was very much alive. I closed my eyes, remembering the days when my spirit had traveled across the heavens. I thought of the peace I had experienced in His presence. Kota was one of the many family members and loved ones I recognized in my time among the one thousand lodge fires.

I breathed deeply and exhaled with a soft sigh. My faith firmly in place…I knew I would see them all again. I loved that I had seen her and our story, in my dreams again.

Chapter 20

Topusana
The Year 2070
One Week Later

I rose from the soft sand of the sleeping chamber and moved toward the bright firelight emanating from the main cavern room.

Several of the council members had gathered around the warmth of the fire. We talked quietly of the days ahead. The excitement of the hunt was palpable. With great anticipation, most longed for and looked forward to the time we spent living out the *old ways*.

It was agreed we would move to the north and west. *"We should reach the buffalo herd within a day or so of travel. The other Bands from the south will join us this day; there will be plentiful meat," Tabba said.*

The others within the circle nodded in agreement. The plan was set. The news of the deaths of the tens of thousands from the foreign army was shocking to other nations worldwide. Others now looked upon our Nation in fear and wonder.

"Perhaps others would not be so bold as to hire armies from across the sea to invade our land," I said.

No additional words were needed.

The People began to gather their traditional weapons and supplies. We began our ascent out of the cavern.

As we exited the cavern into the bright morning sun, hundreds of Comanche and Apache tribal members greeted us. We began our walk toward the north and west. Friends and family sang together as we traveled. Hundreds of horses were brought up by the Warriors, taking their place in the rear of the procession. Dozens of travois rolled along the plain, carrying our teepee lodges. In the distance to the south, we could see the cloud of dust that trailed the other Bands heading in our direction. We would travel slowly, allowing them to close the distance between us. A group of hunters arrived mid-morning amidst a loud rising cheer from *The People*. Within their group were several war ponies loaded with buffalo meat from the first kill.

Tonight, the feast would begin.

****

The Next Morning
The year 2070
3:00 a.m.

The intelligence had been received from Israel. We had three hours.

My satellite phone pinged. The news was unbelievable, incomprehensible.

The word traveled quickly among *The People*. In terror we ran together through the night toward the safety of the cavern system. I observed Tabba in the moonlight to my right. His face strained, intent, he ran at a steady pace holding our young grandsons, one child tucked under each of his strong arms.

These Thousand Days

I too carried our granddaughters, one under each arm as I ran. My arms ached with their weight. My lungs burned at the frantic pace. Peering across the moonlit plain, I could see others running in the silent horror at the news. Where was Little Abigail? I was certain she was close behind.

I prayed in my heart as I ran, thankful we had received a three-hour notice. Time was our enemy now; that we knew. It was fourteen miles of rugged terrain to the cavern entrance. The fall night air was cool and clean as I breathed in deeply and came to a stop for a moment, recovering my wind. Behind me I could see families strung across the prairie for miles. My heart sank. In the distance were hundreds lagging behind the pace.

I knew the older ones were struggling. In my spirit I saw their deaths. In the stillness I heard faintly the songs of death emanating from the rear of our procession. I turned and ran; perhaps I could return for others.

As I raced across the prairie I thought of another time and place. I thought of the night my mother Kwanita had died. The Spaniards had attacked us. We were simply in the way of their pursuit of the Cavalry soldiers. I remembered the run I had made six times carrying the young children into the safety of Palo Duro Canyon. A stillness in the midst of what was soon to occur settled across the prairie. I turned and ran and struggled with all my might. I stumbled while crossing a small dry creek bed, falling to the ground. One of my granddaughters scrapped both knees on the rocky terrain. She began to cry. I gently wiped the blood from her knees. In her face as I attempted to comfort her…I saw the face of my daughter Prairie Song. The memory came to me from across the years. I too began to cry.

Our escape, our run, our songs, our silence, blended into a crescendo of heartache, death, and destruction. *The Numunuu* (The People) were yet again facing genocide.

Upon reaching the cavern entrance we passed our grandchildren into the hands of the Warriors gathered at the small entrance. They would move the little ones deep into the cavern. "Let us return for more, Tabba." I saw the look in his eyes.

"We have eighteen minutes, Sana." I understood.

"Theirs will be a good death, Sana." he said.

"Where is Little Abigail?" I questioned frantically, my heart racing.

****

18 minutes later
6:00 a.m.

The explosion and shock wave ripped across the prairie, creating a force of wind moving in excess of three-hundred miles per hour and air temperatures more than six hundred degrees fahrenheit. The blast zone covered a radius of thirty miles. The low yield nuclear weapon melted the hides of buffalo instantly as tens of thousands of the magnificent creatures boiled into the dust of Mother Earth. The prairie fires would burn for weeks.

Most members of the tribe had moved safely underground. Those who had entered the cavern prior to the explosion were secure and protected…for now. We had no way of knowing the number above ground that had perished. It was painfully obvious to me, many of the most vulnerable, our elderly, and young children had not arrived in time.

My son David consulted with his sources within Israeli intelligence. It would be necessary to stay underground for months…possibly longer.

I gazed into the eyes of my Warrior son William Nica and saw a familiar look.

"Wolf is armed and fully charged, Mother."

"Have you found Little Abigail?" I asked through a veil of tears.

****

In my dreams that night I again *saw* my third born son. Samuel sat by his fire on the edge of the Outback half a world away. His songs came to me, and I sang within my dreams along with him…the song of war. I once again clearly saw the warrior heart that had awakened. Knowing and comfort rested within my soul at this revelation. My son Samuel (Kicking Fox) would now live the life he had been set apart and trained for. His Warrior spirit had finally awakened.

To be continued…

From the Author

My hope is that you have enjoyed this Book 3 Novella: *These Thousand Days*, and the continuing narrative of Topusana and *The People*. My final full-length novel in the A New Beginning Series, Book 4, Kicking Fox, will be published in the fall of 2022. Please watch for updates and release information on my webpage and blog at stevenghightower.com or facebook.com/anewbeginning2020

Thank you for your support and kind reviews.
Steven G. Hightower
April 2022 Alto, New Mexico

Please enjoy the following excerpt from Book 4, Kicking Fox.

Excerpt from Steven G. Hightower's A New Beginning Series

Book 4
KICKING FOX
Prologue

The criminal psychologists had studied the cases for years. Some would conclude Kicking Fox, aka Samuel Nica, was completely sane. Kicking Fox, his preferred name when referenced by the press, was the fierce Warrior and son of renowned Warrior Tabbananica. Others were certain the man was bi-polar, or suffered from some type of brain injury, or tumor, or some yet to be determined psychosis. Others thought him simply a sociopath.

Documentary film producers, and Hollywood moguls analyzed each and every individual case. The movie productions they developed from expert witnesses and the most talented screen writers in the industry, most accurately portrayed the truth of who Kicking Fox was.

These producers and writers accurately replicated what his psyche portrayed. The stories were fascinating, wildly popular, and millions across the globe idolized him.

Governments across the globe were less enamored with the man's activities. He was hunted, located, arrested, charged, and tried across multiple continents…and never found guilty of any crime.

Despite the innocent verdicts, Kicking Fox was a target. He was hunted by governments from across the globe. Killers retained within dark basements on scrambled cell phones were contracted. None were successful, and many were never heard from again.

Some insist that Kicking Fox is dead now. Others claim he is simply waiting in seclusion. Still others believe him to have assumed an unknown identity and living a normal life in an isolated faraway place. The last possibility…he was living in plain sight but somehow had become unrecognizable.

Chapter 1

Kicking Fox

I had seen this happen in other men. It was never something one could put a finger on. A series of events, perhaps the cumulative effect of injustice, whether perceived or real, brought about this radical transformation. Perspective is what was most missing in the breaking of the inner man, perspective that I did not possess nor recognize.

Having witnessed this snap, or breaking, in others, I was surprised I did not immediately recognize the occurrence in my own soul. But it was plainly evident. The event changed the way I thought. The turning point changed my actions and deeds. I was no longer going to remain complacent.

I had had enough.

Just yesterday I had loaded my suitcase, going through the mindless motions of packing. I had done this for decades. Prepare for another long haul. I would be out fifteen days this time. I would touchdown on three continents, cross completely half the time zones on the globe. I placed the mechanical wind-up clock in the suitcase. No digital read out, no battery or solar power, just a wind-up clock with a dial I adjusted daily to whatever time zone I found myself in. I had a secret. A secret to staying fit, alert, and avoiding the jet lag that most travelers suffered from. I simply slept eight hours per day no matter the time zone, continent, or language being spoken. The simple solution worked for me. I was ever alert, my mind keen and aware.

I disassembled the forty-five automatic into its fourteen plastic pieces. Some went into my shaving kit, others into the little compartments of my luggage. The bullets I had just 3D printed last night. Each one composed of one hundred percent high grade plastic. The powder and wad stuffing I hid away into scent proof containers. I would not have any problems with customs. They knew me well. My profile was posted in every database and intelligence agency across the globe.

My ceremonial war club, high grade plastic bow, and the hand-hewn oak arrows, along with sharpened plastic broadheads were tucked away as always into their respective hidden compartments. The plastics of my long knife would never be detected by the metal sensing and X-ray equipment found in most travel terminals. I moved about the world well-armed, unbeknownst to the security teams that surveilled the mass public. I was always prepared. This trip would be no different I told myself. But deep within I sensed I would need and utilize my weapons.

I sat in the crew compartment of the 747-1000 awaiting the first crew's duty time limitations to expire and begin my time as captain. The plan suddenly began to take on shape and form. I detailed each step. My every move I began to scrutinize and perfect.

After a few hours, I began to see not only the plan, but also the changes within my mind. Something within my soul had indeed broken at the news I had received from my brother William just four hours into my flight. My life…would never be the same.

These Thousand Days

****

"Captain Nica, can I get you anything?" Sally Wolf peered deep into my eyes with a questioning look that contained much more than refreshments in her offer. I breathed deeply, remembering the last trip. The beach, the smell of the ocean, the taste of oysters, and fresh crab…along with the taste of Sally herself. I smiled. "I'm good, Sally." With a wink she moved forward to the cockpit. Her movements were graceful, even sensual. Sally Wolf of the great Shoshone tribe was a stunningly beautiful woman. I tried not to stare.

She returned a few moments later. "Will you be laying over in Sydney?" A longing in her perfectly sculpted face permeated her question.

"Yes," I answered honestly. "But I'm sorry, Sally, I have some business to attend to this time." I saw instantly the hurt in her eyes. The last thing I wanted to do was hurt her. I had no words to explain what I was about to do. She touched me on the shoulder as she moved toward the service area. I felt the electricity at her touch, followed by the definitive manly stirrings in my soul. I breathed deeply again. Would her comfort, her love, her beauty, ever be mine again?

There was no answer to that internal question posed within my mind. I would need to plan and execute my steps flawlessly. Sally would be much safer not knowing.

Chapter 2

The coastline of Australia appeared as we descended out of the broken overcast at 5,000 feet msl (mean sea level). In a few moments, the massive runways of Sydney Airport filled the windscreen of our 747-1000 as we ran the final landing checklists. I focused on the checklist tasks at hand, and at one thousand feet agl (above ground level), I disconnected the autoland system. I adjusted to the slight cross wind that swept in from Botany Bay across runway 34L. The aircraft was relatively light now at just under 600,000 pounds after burning fourteen hours of fuel. Still, airspeed and altitude control would need to be precise. My co-pilot called out those speeds in succinct progression. I corrected, slightly lifting the nose of the massive aircraft and reducing the power by 10 percent. The pleasant woman's voice programed into the autopilot dutifully began altitude call outs. I eased the power off again as the automated voice announced, "one hundred feet." "Just let her settle," I said aloud. "Fifty feet." I held her nose high. "Twenty…ten…" Two seconds later the huge main landing gear made contact with the surface. I applied a little left rudder as the ship attempted to yaw into the wind. She straightened as I gently lowered the nose. Upon contact of the nose gear with the runway surface, I brought the enormous engines into full reverse as 600,000 pounds of aircraft, fuel, and cargo from across the globe began to decelerate.

I suppose no matter how many times this task of landing safely and bringing to a stop a machine of this size and complexity is undertaken, the outcome is never certain until the aircraft rests within the chocked wheels at a proper gate with its engines shut down. It would take another twenty minutes of checklists, taxiing through the web of complex runway intersections, and following ground control instructions before eventually we came to a stop. I breathed deeply and relaxed my grip on the power levers as the engines slowly spooled down. A few minutes of paperwork, acknowledgments from my fellow crewmembers on a nice flight and landing, then I was off. My mission clear. I would not report back after the two-day layover in Sydney. This would be my last flight. I knew I would eventually make my way back to the United States, and back to the reservation in New Mexico where I was born. It might take months or even years for that to happen. I focused my thoughts on the task at hand. When a man breaks, he begins to see the events of the future clearly, events that might motivate a change in the way governments and world leaders behave.

Yes, I was certain my actions would cause some to consider their motives and the paths to power they were willing to take. Sometimes a bully, or a tyrant, a dictatorial political thief, simply needs to be called to account.

The meeting was set to take place in two weeks. Fourteen days of the ticking clock commenced now. Though not on the invitation list, I would be in attendance at this meeting.

Chapter 3

Two Years Earlier
New Mexico

I stood alone along the edge of the grave. Little streams of dirt drifting from under my feet into the dark hole before me. She was too young. This should not have happened. The remains of my seven-year-old daughter contained in the casket at my feet held nothing but an empty shell. The decomposing body that previously housed the most beautiful spirit I had ever met no longer held that spirit. Prairie Wind was gone. Her spirit, I knew, was in heaven, or the great land, or paradise. Whatever belief others, or my people, put their faith in, or hoped for, whatever seed of faith gave a person hope, I possessed. I knew without doubt such a kind, innocent, caring spirit that was my daughter was long departed. I also understood in my own spirit Prairie Wind was now in the presence of her mother and all our loved ones that had fallen asleep. She was now loved and free from the hurt and pain of this world.

Two funerals inside of one month. I observed the stone marker with her mother's name engraved along its glossy granite face. *"I miss you, Ela."* The Apache meaning of my late wife's name was *Earth*. I thought how ironic that seemed as I stood near her grave within the earth. *"I do not understand why you have both left me."* I turned and walked away in silence.

Looking back, it was without a doubt that day the breaking of my soul began. It is difficult to describe this darkening, this cloud of hatred or vengeance that might consume one's own mind and purpose. It was a seed of darkness planted firmly within the injustice that lay at the bottom of my daughter's grave. I knew that day someone would pay for her life, or the life that she would never live out. Someone.

The company promptly grounded me. Human resources would never allow a captain to continue his work after the death of a family member. At the death of a loved one, mandatory grief counseling and psychological evaluations were ordered. It would take months for me to complete the required training…or indoctrination might have been a better description. They wanted to make certain the seed that had been planted at the gravesite of my wife and daughter never blossomed and grew. Those in power both within the company and without, specifically the government, would make certain I would be a good little Indian. Compliant, mindless, willing to drink the Kool-Aid.

After a full year, the powers that be decided I would comply. I was given a reduced schedule at first. And I was watched. The surveillance videos recorded every word and movement. Every flight was analyzed, every conversation reviewed. Somewhere in the depths of the inner workings of the largest airline in the world, a psychologist pronounced me fit. I would resume a normal flight schedule. The surveillance would end.

But they had missed something. Something that their careful observation and psychological evaluations could never reveal. In my heart I was a Warrior, trained by my grandfather Tenahpu in the *Old Ways,* and I, Samuel Nica, Kicking Fox, would not comply. I would make certain those responsible for the death of my loved ones, would pay…with their own lives.

I thought it odd or even comical that the question that might reveal the most about me, was never asked. That type of question had it been posed, in all the political correctness, posturing and analytical testing, that one question might have been quite revealing. It may have been difficult to conceal my true Warrior heart. But they never asked about vengeance, or revenge, and it would be mine.

****

Present Day

I made my way along within the massive structure of Sydney Airport, eventually exiting into the smog-filled air of the underground garage. The van driver was pleasant as I allowed him to load my bags into the rear of the courtesy van. The drive to the hotel was filled with expletives and confused honking of horns as the snarl of traffic that engulfed us eventually made its way onto the freeway. My mind wandered at the mass of humanity surrounding me. I longed for the wildness of the back country. I closed my eyes, imagining the high mountains of my homeland so far away in New Mexico. It was winter there now. I could feel the cold and smell the fresh snow-laden air. What had I become? I wondered. In my past I had longed to escape the Rez.

I desired something different, even some level of success in the modern world that was not available within my homeland.

I had climbed this ladder of achievement only to realize in this very moment…none of what I was living and surrounded by mattered. The airports, whether in Europe, or South

America, or here in Australia, were all exactly the same. The hotels identical in location, room appointments, even linens, lighting, and window placement. The restaurants served the same food and wine across the globe. So many days and nights I had spent in these places, and upon awakening, many of those early mornings it was impossible to determine where I was. Some days I had to consult my flight data or smart phone to establish whether I was in Paris, Dallas Fort Worth, or London. Maybe what I had desired and chased for years now was a complete waste of time.

The driver spoke to me again. "Sir, are you alright?" We had stopped, the door was open as he awaited my exit from the van.

"Sure, um, I'm good, just a little jet lag." He looked at me curiously. I would need to be much more careful. I could not allow even the slightest questions as to my mental acuity. He smiled in understanding. "I get that, Captain, made the trip across the pond myself a time or two. Not sure how you pilots deal with the time zone changes. Have a pleasant stay." The young man handed my bags over. I tipped him nicely and nodded.

"Nothing a couple of days on the beach won't cure," I said smiling.

"Now you're talking my language, mate," he said with a strong Ausie accent. "Enjoy your layover." And with that he was quickly back in the driver seat, honking at the departing traffic.

I was certain he would not recall anything unusual about our conversation. It would be a full month before the police would question him about our ride from the airport.

I checked in at the front desk to the cheerful smiles and distinct friendly accent of a beautiful blond-haired, blue-eyed

Australian desk attendant. I politely declined the offer for assistance with my luggage and made my way to the requested secluded room on the 24th floor of the massive building. I had much planning to do, but I needed rest for now. I darkened the room, covering all windows with the heavy drapery. I assembled my plastic forty-five automatic and laid it on my nightstand. I then lit a small candle and set flame to the delicate bundle of sacred incense I always carried with me. I breathed in deeply the scent that took me to another place and time.

I spent a full hour in my "time of quiet" as my grandfather had instructed me. He had trained me well. My quiet time would be vital in my planning and strategy over the next two weeks. Resolve settled within my heart and mind as I drifted into a deep sleep.

Chapter 4

Eight hours later the alarm sounded on the little wind-up clock. I needed the rest and had slept peacefully. I opened the curtains as the sun was setting across Sydney harbor, the sky filled with vibrant hues of orange and pink. It was morning back in the high mountains of New Mexico. There, the sun would be rising in the east, as the sun set here outside my window half a world away. I took a deep breath. I felt the incredible distance to my homeland from here… both physically and emotionally. I whispered aloud, "Have I gotten too far from you, my mountains…to ever make my way home?" The voice of my woman, Ela, my daughter, and my people answered from across the heavens. I breathed deeply again, now knowing the answer I earnestly sought.

The plan was beginning to take shape in my mind. I knew the importance of seeing my steps and actions in my mind… before living them out. Wisdom is what I would seek in every detail, movement, and decision. I punched the contact as my cell phone dialed the number to airline operations. It would be wise to buy some time.

"Captain Nica reporting in."

"Good morning, Captain. Good to hear from you. I have you departing tomorrow at 07:00. You'll have a short layover in Anchorage, and then on to Chicago." I could hear the sound of a keyboard busily typing. "And then it looks like you're home for a couple of weeks. Is that still correct?"

"I'm actually a little under the weather. Seems like maybe bad food last night, no other symptoms other than gastrointestinal. I think it best for me to not fly tomorrow." The silence on the other end of the line hung awkwardly for a moment. Would they dismiss this, a minor intestinal issue? I knew the policies; they would act swiftly.

"I'll need to send the testing team to you within the hour."

"It's really pretty obvious to me it's not the virus, but whatever you think best." I said, feigning innocence.

"Please remain in your room, Captain. The testing team is on the way and should arrive within the hour."

"Understood." I said as I ended the call. The plan was unfolding exactly as I had hoped. The test results would arrive on my smart phone two hours later. All virus scans were negative. I, however, would be quarantined for a full seven days. How many days would it be before they discovered I was no longer in my room was a question for which I did not have the answer. But I knew I had bought myself some time. I felt a twinge of guilt, knowing the crew and passengers from my last flight would also be traced and placed in quarantine. I thought of Sally. I would need to learn to set aside any emotions of guilt, even the slightest twinge.

I plugged my phone into the charger and made certain it was on and all location tracking was activated. I knew they would monitor my whereabouts continuously. The authorities had delivered a large box of dehydrated food and several cases of water. By now the door to my room would be bolted and locked from the outside. The instructions were clear and succinct, I would not be allowed to leave the room for seven days.

I loaded my weapons, a few of the freeze-dried meals and several water bottles into the small lightweight pack. I dressed in my exercise sweats, running shoes, light jacket, and ball cap. I would become just another tourist out for an evening jog.

I removed the vent cover and crawled through the small ducting into the adjacent room. I forced the vent cover off in the adjacent room with a swift kick and lowered myself to the floor. I repeated the same removing of vent covers and crawling through the air conditioning vents for seven full rooms. Hoping I was far enough away from the cameras that would be trained outside the door to my room, I exited far down the hallway from where I was supposed to be. The cameras recorded someone leaving the room I exited on the 24th floor. None of the security teams noticed the movement. That footage would not be viewed for over a week.

I made my way out of the hotel via a service elevator and kitchen delivery entrance. The city was just coming alive. The streets were busy with steady traffic; the bars and restaurants were filling with patrons. I began to run, moving north and west, I knew exactly where I was going. One of the largest uninhabited geographic regions remaining on the planet, the Australian Outback.

****

One hour later the traffic began to thin. I took to one of the numerous side roads leading away from the city and slowed to a walk. The sun had fully set and the glow of the city behind me dampened the starlight overhead. I needed one critical tool before leaving the city behind. I scanned the horizon, then turned toward the brightest glow remaining in the night sky. I walked briskly in the direction of the lights and soon spotted exactly what I was looking for. The strip mall contained a variety of quaint shops and boutiques. I pulled my ballcap low over my brow and tucked my hands into my pockets. I was certain my skin tone was undetectable to the surveillance cameras. I took a few moments to select the best non-contract sat phone available. I paid with cash, grateful that I had used an ATM in the States prior to my departure. I exited with my head held low, intentionally never looking into a camera or toward any person.

Once away from the quickly fading lights of Sydney, Australia, I began to run again. One hour later I sat in the bush along the edge of the beginnings of the Outback. The night sky was ablaze with starlight, constellations, even the Southern Cross showed its majesty high in the vast stellar space. I chanced a small fire and again entered into my time of quiet. The voices of my ancestors filled my heart and mind. The voices of the innocent called out from across time. Those among my people who had been massacred centuries ago called to me. The voices of those eliminated by the creation of the viruses and resulting deaths these weapons had caused whispered into my heart and mind.

Lastly the voices of my wife and my daughter…called to me from across the veil that lies between the unseen spirit world and the seen physical world we who are alive inhabit. The voices sang their death songs. They sang a new song representing the throngs that had been eliminated. My heart broke again at the stark realization and truth that my wife and daughter had departed this world at the hand of evil. The reaction within their bodies had been brutal. The suffering beyond what any human should ever endure. They had died alone. No loved ones allowed anywhere near their lonely torturous isolation. The new vaccines had taken three full days to kill my loved ones.

I sat in the bush alongside my little fire and read again the message I had received from my brother William on my satellite phone less than twenty-four hours ago.

"Deploy Wolf north and west, Red Army!"

My Homeland had been attacked; it was for me the last injustice imposed upon my people in a long and sordid history of injustice…that I would ever allow to occur without consequences.

Perhaps, I wondered, if *breaking* was the wrong term to describe what I had experienced in the last several hours. Perhaps an *awakening* was a better term.

****

I dreamed of my mother that night. Topusana Nica, Akima (Leader) of our people, was the bravest person I had ever known. Yes, she was my mother and my attachment to her as a son left a bond that was unbreakable. However, the closeness and communion I felt that night half a world away from her was incomprehensible. A communication took place between us across Mother Earth, across oceans, across the time zones. She knew.

She knew of the choice I had made, and the awakening that had occurred within my Warrior spirit.

Steven G. Hightower

Made in the USA
Columbia, SC
27 August 2022